STRENGTH WITHIN

MIA BARNES

STRENGTH WITHIN

MIA BARNES

Affinity
Rainbow Publications

2024

Strength Within
© 2024 by Mia Barnes

Affinity E-Book Press NZ LTD.
Canterbury, New Zealand

Edition First (1st)

ISBN: 978-1-99-104061-9 (paperback)
ISBN: 978-1-99-104062-6 (EPUB)
ISBN: 978-1-99-104063-3 (PDF)
ISBN: 978-1-99-104064-0 (KINDLE)

All rights reserved.

Editor: A Koenig
Proof Editor: Lisa M
Cover Design: Irish Dragon Designs
Production Design: Affinity Publication Services

ACKNOWLEDGMENTS

My tribe…you never let me stop believing in me. None of this would have been possible without y'all! Thank you for always being in my corner! A huge thank you to Annette Mori for her mentorship. What I've learned from you is invaluable. I will forever be grateful for you and the knowledge gained. Another huge thank you to Affinity for this opportunity…. it feels like home. To all the readers and authors who have taken the time to wish me the best. Thank you for your support!

DEDICATION

I dedicate this novel to all the strong women out there who don't give up, no matter how difficult it gets!

TABLE OF CONTENTS

PROLOGUE

Milwaukee, Wisconsin

June 2015

Let me tell your story, and let's make it a happy ending.

My name is Samantha Wilson and telling other people's stories isn't just what I do—it's my passion. I've met many inspirational young women who have survived some of the worst cases of domestic violence. They still shine and become a beacon for others. Their strength is inspiring. They don't want to be seen as victims or allow it to be what defines them. For me, it is always an honor to tell their stories.

There was a time when I had no voice and I felt alone. Being a writer allows me to be the voice of those who haven't found theirs yet. It also allows me to bring awareness to a sickening crisis that plagues our society on many levels. Too many young women are affected by this evil, often hidden in our communities' underlying layers. As a writer, I aim to expose these layers and help end this hell on earth for so many young women. I want them to know they're not alone.

I came to Milwaukee to work on an investigative story with my former colleague. Brian asked me to join him because of my previous work with young women who were victims of domestic violence. It seems the story is about a fake rehab center that is part of something bigger. It may be a major trafficking operation, with hundreds of girls of all ages. Brian and I will meet on Monday to go over the details.

CHAPTER ONE

The Assignment

Before arriving in Wisconsin, I found a quaint little house in Shorewood, a small suburb north of Milwaukee. It was a perfect place for me to stay. The house was located a mile east of Lake Michigan and a few miles west of the Milwaukee River. It reminded me of a place that was once my happy space. My grandparents' home had been on the shore, about an hour north of Shorewood, and was full of warmth and happy childhood memories, unlike the others I tried to forget. The ones that came from the hell I left long ago.

The first day was rainy and a perfect day to stay inside. Bella seemed to agree and slept most of the day away at my feet. She was my traveling buddy and loyal companion, a heeler mix I had adopted a few months earlier. There were days when her persistence was what got me out the door and away from my laptop for some exercise. I walked out onto the small deck and could smell the beach in the air. Summer in Wisconsin is the best time of the year. It was odd being back in the area. I hadn't been back since my grandfather's funeral. At first, I wasn't going to take the assignment because I had vowed never to return. My grandparents were the only reason I ever went back, and they were both gone. The rest of my family hated me after an incident that took so much from me. There were a lot of memories I never wanted to recall, but the assignment was an important story, so I went anyway.

I walked back into the house, and Bella came running up to me. She was ready for our walk. As we strolled along the riverside, the squirrels chatted and frolicked around us as if trying to provoke Bella. She paid no attention to them as she pranced down the path beside me. Our daily walks were always enjoyable and a great way to reboot.

As another walker approached, she struggled with her little Pomeranian, who appeared to want a piece of Bella. I smiled at her, and we both laughed.

"Good morning," I said.

"Good morning," she replied.

The parks were well maintained, and the flower beds were flawless, with great layouts of beautiful blooms. People were walking through with their family or their dogs.

I sat on a bench to take in the park and the beautiful morning—the surrounding flower beds filled with red monarda, daylilies, lilies, phlox, and sedums. As I took in the fragrance, it reminded me of early mornings with my grandma as she weeded her flower beds. Especially the sweet scent of the phlox, her favorite flower.

Small ponds at the bottom of the hill had colorful fish of orange and yellow, with lily pads and waterlilies. I heard the river behind me as the water splashed against rocks on its path between the banks that held it in. I could've stayed in this spot forever, taking in the surrounding beauty. But I had things to do, and Bella was letting me know she was ready to go, too.

†

Monday morning, Brian and I met at a coffee shop in Shorewood. We sat at a table across from each other, laptops in front of us. He started to tell me about the rehab center.

"So, what we know so far is that the director has no formal education or licensing. The therapist is the same; as it turns out, she's his girlfriend. They run an extensive sex trafficking ring out of rehab and group homes."

"Damn, how do they pull that off? And for how long?" I asked.

"They believe it started as a legitimate rehab program when it opened in 1995. It appears the current director took over in 2003, which is around the time the sex trafficking began. This goes much deeper, and there are a lot of girls involved."

"How young are we talking?" I asked.

"Twelve years old is the youngest, from my understanding."

I gasped. "Oh my God, that is horrible. When will the authorities get those girls out of there?"

"They've been investigating for months now and had undercover agents working in the homes and rehab center. They're getting ready to bust it open. But they haven't moved in yet because they need to have all appropriate warrants in hand to do so."

"How much longer will these girls have to live in this hell?"

"Not long. The people working on this are pushing it through as fast as possible," he said.

"I certainly hope so. There is no hell like the hell they are in right now."

"How do you feel about staying a while?"

"I'm here for as long as it takes. I hope they will act swiftly for those girls," I said.

It hurt my soul to think of those young women living in that situation.

"So tell me, what is my role?" I asked Brian.

"A young woman came in as a Jane Doe at a Milwaukee hospital a few weeks ago. She was in bad shape and unconscious but later identified as one of the girls from the group homes operated by the same people from the rehab center. She woke up a few days ago, afraid to talk to anyone."

"Can't blame her," I said.

I closed my laptop. Brian was giving me this look like he wanted to ask me something.

"What is it, Brian? Just ask me already."

"Would you interview her?" he asked.

"What makes you think she'll trust me or even want to talk to me?"

"Because, Sammie, you have this way with people, a kindness that just makes people feel comfortable."

"I don't know about all that, Brian, but I'll try. I'm not going to promise anything. I'll meet with her, and we can go from there. I'm not going to push her to talk to me."

"Of course. Just do that thing you do, Sammie." He smiled at me.

I rolled my eyes at him. "Where can I meet Jane Doe?"

"I'll text you with that information and keep you updated on what's happening with the rehab center and homes.

"Thank you, Brian. I'll keep you updated, too."

†

The following morning, I headed to the hospital. Despite Brian's confidence in me, I wasn't sure showing up in a scared young woman's room was the best way to try and connect with her. I've interviewed many girls who have been through hell, but their parents or a loved one was with them. The girl known as Jane Doe was alone and scared, so I wanted to talk to the only person I knew she had a connection with at that time.

I scheduled a meeting with Jane Doe's case manager, who had been with her from the day she was admitted. She would be restricted by HIPPA regulations from sharing information with me, I understood that, but I wanted to see what the best approach would be to meet with the young lady. Whose name I'd learned was Lexi.

†

The lady at the front desk in the hospital lobby smiled at me as I approached her window. "Good morning. Can I help you?"

"Ah yes, I'm here to see Janet Metcalf. I have a ten o'clock appointment."

"I'll let her know you are here."

The case manager met me at the front desk, we shook hands, and I introduced myself.

"I'm Samantha Wilson. We spoke yesterday."

"Yes, nice to meet you. I'm Janet."

We walked to her office to talk. "So, what brings you here, Ms. Wilson?"

"I'm a writer here in Milwaukee to work on a story. It involved one of your patients. They asked me to meet with the young lady that was brought in as Jane Doe."

The look on her face made it seem as if she wasn't a fan of the idea.

"Look, I know this girl has been through hell. I'm not here to make it any worse for her. To be honest, right now, I'm not here for the story, I'm here for her. The people I work with know this." I paused. "I understand she hasn't done a lot of talking."

"Yeah, she is extremely withdrawn. She will respond to my questions with a yes or no. Her friend does most of the talking for her. "

"Her friend?" I asked.

"Yes, she is quite different. She likes to talk. If they're together they seem to be comfortable. We can give it a try and see if they respond to you."

"It makes me feel better knowing she has someone with her."

"Me, too."

Janet explained there was a connection between the two of them, but she couldn't give me personal information. I'd find out later that the friend had been in the hospital around the same time, with what could've been a fatal infection in her uterus. They said that she saw Lexi one day when the nurses were wheeling her through the hall, and she refused to leave her side. Staff later figured out they were from the same girls' home and moved them into a room together.

I filled Janet in on the story we were working on and the reason I wanted to meet with Lexi. Neither one of us was sure of how they would react, but Janet was someone they felt safe with. She agreed to introduce me to the young ladies, and I assured her I'd only stay if they were comfortable with me.

We walked to Lexi's room, and I followed Janet's lead.

"Hello ladies," she said.

"Hi, Janet." The girl with Lexi said as she looked around her to see me. "Who's that with you?"

"She is here to visit with you if you're okay with that."

"What's your name?" Lexi's friend asked me.

"My name is Samantha Wilson."

The girls looked at each other, and the young lady said, "This is Lexi, and I'm, well, everyone calls me Lou."

"It's nice to meet both of you."

"Why do you want to visit with us?" Lou asked.

"Well, I'm a writer and I'm here in Milwaukee working on a story." I paused. "When I met with my colleague yesterday, he told me how brave you both were, and I wanted to meet you myself."

"Lexi is my friend. She is the bravest."

"I'm glad you have each other. Friends are very important."

Janet stepped forward. "Ladies, I need to get back to work. Would you be okay with Ms. Wilson staying for a while?"

Lou looked at Lexi again. They both shrugged their shoulders and then Lou said, "Sure. She can stay."

"Okay, ladies, if you need anything, you know you can call me anytime."

"Bye, Janet," Lou said. Her eyes were sizing me up it seemed. I felt like I was about to get some serious questions from Lou.

"Thank you, Janet," I said. She smiled at me.

"Do you mind if I have a seat?" I asked.

"You can sit over there." Lou pointed at the loveseat under the window.

I walked over and sat down. The old ugly curtains on the window behind me were closed most of the way.

"What's your name again?" Lou asked.

"You can call me Sammie or Sam."

"Sammie, why you want to talk to us?" Lou asked.

"Because I admire brave young women like you and Lexi."

"What kind of stories do you write?" She asked.

"I write different stories for magazines and newspapers. Mostly I write stories about amazing young women."

"Why do you care about people like us?" Those were the first words Lexi spoke.

"Why wouldn't I care?" I asked.   Silence.

I saw Lexi's face go soft, and a tear tried to fall, but she abruptly wiped it away.

Lou broke the silence. "If I tell you my story, will you write about it? And can it have a happy ending?"

"Of course. Let's make it a happy ending."

I didn't want to overstay my welcome, and I could tell Lexi wasn't entirely comfortable with me being there. I stood and walked toward the girls. Handing both one of my cards, I smiled at Lexi.

"You can call me anytime," I said.

"Can you stay for a while longer?" Lou asked.

"Of course, if Lexi is okay with me staying," I said.

"Lexi?" Lou asked her.

"Yeah, it's okay," she whispered.

I walked over to the loveseat and sat down. Lou did most of the talking, and you could tell she needed someone to hear her, so I listened as she talked. She told me about her parents' death. A car accident that took them when she was only ten years old. The authorities separated her from her little sister and put her in the system. She was twenty-two years old now and had been in that hell for many years. Finding her sister and getting her GED is what she told me would bring her a happy ending. As she talked, I saw how her face light up when she told me about getting an apartment with Lexi and the other things she wanted to do.

Hope. I saw it in her eyes. The healing had begun. It would take time to overcome the impact of years of abuse, but she was in a great place now. She was a comfort to Lexi, and without Lou, I doubt any connection would happen for me.

Lexi was withdrawn and avoided eye contact as much as possible. From the little I knew about her, she never had a solid parent. It must have been difficult to trust anyone because no one had ever been there to keep her safe. It wasn't hard to imagine being abused, neglected, or rejected by the ones that were supposed to be there and keep such children safe. For some, they survived by going numb and disconnecting from any emotion or feeling. It pissed their inner child off and they weren't gonna trust just anyone that walked into their space. I understood that, and I had heard the stories, some of which rattled my soul—part of me listened because they wanted someone to hear them. I wrote because people needed to understand that the cycle must end.

As Lou continued to talk, Lexi would occasionally glance my way. Her eyes were so dark, surrounded by the fresh scars from a life she didn't choose. She looked scared, and she probably had a lot of walls up. It would take some time before she would let me in.

†

They transferred Lexi to the rehabilitation wing to begin therapy about a month after our first visit. I saw her often, and she seemed to like our visits. I let her lead our conversations. She wasn't ready to talk about what had happened yet, and I wasn't going to press it.

One day, I was pushing Lexi's wheelchair as we returned to her room after a grueling physical therapy session.

Out of nowhere, she said, "I want to tell you my story, Sammie."

I stopped in front of her room. "Are you sure, Lexi?"

"Yes." She looked at me. "I'm sure."

"Okay."

†

I arranged for us to have a small table in a private dining room at the hospital. As I sat across from Lexi, her courage and strength were inspiring. It'd been many weeks since she was admitted to the hospital as a Jane Doe with horrible and extensive injuries. She had been through multiple surgeries, and her transformation came in baby steps, but it was noticeable to me, just in the few weeks I had known her.

The scar next to her right eye had faded, and the multiple knife wounds were doing the same. Her broken bones were healing, too, and she continued to get stronger in physical therapy. There were times she would smile at me with the face of a twenty-three-year-old girl with hope. But other times, the burden on her mind and soul from the years of mental abuse was still transparent through her big brown eyes.

Her story was one of the toughest I had ever listened to. She told me how it all started.

"My mom worked two jobs, sometimes three, because my stepfather refused to work. While she was at work, he would drug me and sexually abuse me. It happened every day, and there was no one to tell," she said as she looked down at the table.

I wanted to tell her to hold her head up because she was better than what happened to her. I could see the shame in the way she held herself. But how do you tell someone this was not their fault when they felt like it was?

I reached out my hand, and she took it. At that moment, I wanted to tell her how sorry I was that no one had been there for her. Instead, I just held her hand.

After a few moments, she continued, "One evening, he never came to my room. I peeked out my bedroom door and saw him passed out on the couch. I grabbed my bag and went out the bedroom window. A friend of mine told me about this place where one of her friends went after she left her parent's house. She gave me the address one day at school because I told her I needed to get away from my house." Lexi paused. Her expression went blank, and I wondered if reflecting on the memories was becoming too much. But then she continued, "I don't remember much after I got there. The people always drugged us before taking us to a new place. When we returned home, we did what the woman said we had to do. When the man got home, we had to go to our rooms. He came to my room to have sex. Sometimes he brought friends, and we had sex with them, too. We couldn't go outside. It wasn't allowed. The last time we were supposed to move, I tried to escape, but they caught me, which is when they stabbed and beat me. Then I woke up in the hospital."

Lexi had escaped her stepfather's world and inadvertently found herself in the middle of the sex trafficking ring. She thought she was going somewhere safe, a place for girls like her. But it was not safe, and they forced her to shoot up meth and heroin. She went dark and did what was necessary to survive.

I learned that the night she left her home, her stepfather didn't pass out. He died of an overdose. Lexi never saw her mother again, and no one ever came looking for her or reported her missing. She was a lost girl in a dangerous world. It had been months since they left her at the hospital. Her freedom came so horrifically, but that day marked the beginning of her life, a life she chose.

Her incredible spirit and unbelievable drive to overcome what had happened amazed me. She was a brave survivor, and she would inspire a lot of people with her courage— including me.

"I don't want to be a victim of what happened to me because it has happened to so many more than just me. It's my goal to help others, not be a victim. I want to help stop these people, too, so they can't hurt anyone else," Lexi insisted.

This assignment had started as a collaboration with a former colleague and had turned into much more. Lexi wanted to tell her story, and the magazine I freelanced for was looking for a feature story for their fall issue. After talking to Lexi, I emailed the magazine, suggested her story, and they agreed it was perfect.

†

A few days later, Bella and I headed out for our morning walk. I needed a distraction because my mind was in overdrive as I thought of all those girls that had been living in this hell for years. The girls were still there as the

Mia Barnes

authorities waded through the red tape to get the warrants. They had to go in all at once, or they could put some of the young women at risk. I'd never been very patient, and I couldn't imagine what the girls went through every day they were left there. Did they feel hopeless as the days went by, wondering if anyone would ever save them or if they were even worthy of being saved? *No one should ever have to feel that way.*

Perhaps that was why I felt connected to Lexi and drawn to telling her story. I had spent my life thinking I wasn't worthy of many things, mostly love.

Bella barked at a squirrel and startled me. We walked to my favorite spot to take in the sights and sounds, and she lay by my feet. It was so beautiful there and not what I remembered about the area. I never took the time to see the beauty because I was always running away from my childhood and the things that happened at that farm just thirty miles north.

Suddenly my thoughts stopped when I heard, "Hey, Sam."

I looked up and saw Lexi walking on the paved path, with a young woman. She still used the walker but was doing great.

"Hey, Lexi." I stood and hugged her. "It's good to see you here."

"Thank you. I love this park," she said.

"Me, too!"

"Who is this?" Lexi asked as she looked at Bella.

"This is Bella,"

"Well, hello, Bella," Lexi said.

Bella's butt started wiggling as she was excited to meet someone new.

Lexi put her hand on the young lady with her and said, "This is my friend, Lanie, she is going to be one of our new roommates when we move into the new place. She walks with me every day."

"Nice to meet you, Lanie. I'm Sam," I said. I reached out my hand to shake hers.

"You, too," she replied.

"When do you get to move into your new place?"

"Soon." She smiled.

The smile on her face made my heart happy. "Lexi, I am so proud of you, girl. You are going to rock life." I gave her another hug. "Well, we need to get back to the house, but it was so good to see you."

Bella and I walked back to the house. My mind contemplated my work as my eyes took in all the beautiful sights we passed on the way. Being back in Wisconsin was strange, and I got a weird vibe. Hesitant at first, I decided to extend my stay because I felt like I was supposed to be there and was meant to meet Lexi and tell her story. The nagging feeling probably came from being close to where my life began.

The one story I couldn't bring myself to tell. My story.

CHAPTER TWO

The Visit

I hoped the investigation would have already led to the closing of the rehab center, group homes, and the arrest of all the responsible people. Brian assured me it was nearing an end. As more information came forth through exploration, there were a lot of twists and turns, which set back plans to go in and make the bust. A judge who had court-ordered rehab for many of the girls was involved in the illegal operation.

Lexi and Lou told me about a "secret door" at the rehab center that led to a place where the older girls were forced to engage in sexual acts with wealthy men. Some were auctioned off and sent to homes to live as sexual servants.

The group homes were revolving doors for men who secretly went there to act on their sick and twisted desires. I wanted those people locked up and the group homes closed. I couldn't help but think of these girls every day, and every morning I hoped that would be the day.

When I wasn't working, I looked for ways to let my mind and body reboot. Bella and I hiked as often as possible. Spending time in nature and being surrounded by its beauty had always brought me inner peace.

Being a tourist was one of my favorite things. I took a tour of a lighthouse, walking step by step up the spiral staircase to the lantern room at the top that housed the bright light and lens. A door led to a narrow platform that went around the outside of the lantern room, where a brave soul could have a fantastic view. I wasn't that brave soul. The man that led the tour told us they called it the widows' walk because sailors' wives would stand on the platform to watch for their husbands' ships to return. Kudos to them.

I went down the spiral staircase. Just outside the lighthouse was an old foundation where a house once stood, the home for the keeper and his family. The house was lost to a fierce storm decades ago after the coast guard decommissioned the lighthouse.

Lighthouses held a special place in my heart. My grandma loved the shore. Her home and garden were full of various miniature lighthouses she had collected. When I went there and spent time on the shore, I felt closer to her.

The following day, Bella and I went hiking before the heat arrived. It was a typical steamy August day in Wisconsin with a lot of humidity. Above-average temperatures were predicted for that summer. We only went a couple of miles because the air was so heavy. As soon as I got home, I jumped in the shower to wash off all the dirt the sweat had attracted. Not to mention the sticky bug spray I had to put on because the mosquitos seemed to like my blood. I threw on some comfy clothes and headed to the living room.

On my way through the kitchen, I grabbed my laptop off the bar and planted myself on the couch. I was ready to tackle my Outlook inbox, which was overflowing with emails. Before I even got a chance to open one, the phone rang.

When I picked up the phone and saw it was Brian, I quickly answered.

"Sam, you're gonna want to get to the police station. It's finally all coming together. They're executing a warrant at the facility and all the homes."

"What? Are you serious? When?" I asked as I quickly stood.

"Now!" He paused. "They will be bringing everyone to the downtown station to book them. I thought you might want to be here," he said.

"Hell yeah, I do. I'm gonna change and I'll be there," I said.

†

Parking was impossible when I arrived downtown. I pulled into the first spot I found and started running toward the station. There were hundreds of people gathering around the police building.

How did all these people know?

Brian called my cell phone.

"Dude, where did all these people come from?" I asked.

"I don't know. It's crazy. Where are you?"

"Walking toward the front entrance," I said.

"Ok, good. Do you have your badge?"

"Yes, of course."

"Show it to the uniforms by the front drive, and they'll let you in."

"Okay, see you in a minute," I said.

There was a barrier between the crowd and the building. Nearby was a circle drive at the front entrance. Police had the driveways closed off to the public, and police cars were lining the streets as they pushed the crowd back. They were blocking off the path for the vehicles carrying the newfound criminals would take.

Trying to get through the crowd was difficult. People backed into me and pushed me around as I made my way through the group. I reached the driveway and flashed my name badge at them, and they motioned for me to come through. Once I made my way into the building, I spotted Brian waving at me. I held up my hand to let him know I saw him and headed his way.

"Wow, so I wasn't expecting all that." I straightened my shirt and ran my fingers through my hair. "You could've warned me, and I would have worn running shoes instead of these sandals."

He laughed. "I don't think anyone was expecting this."

"How did all these people find out?"

"They think someone leaked information, and the story hit Facebook as the news crews showed up at the rehab center." He shook his head. "By 9:30 this morning, the crowds started moving in, and they had to block the roads off so they could back them up to get the vehicles through."

"It's nuts, for sure. So, what is the plan?" I asked.

"We'll park ourselves right by the door, and they'll walk the suspects through to booking."

"So, we get front row?" I asked.

"Yes." He smiled and then pointed at a guy with him. "He'll be doing a live Facebook feed on our page."

"Nice," I said.

I had to admit there was some joy running through my heart and soul as I prepared to watch them lead those monsters to their new life.

Soon we heard the crowd break into cheers. They started by leading the rogue little bald man and his ratchet girlfriend by us. He looked like he was sweating a bit, and she had makeup running down her face in a trail from her meaningless tears. The judge got out of the back of a police car, and the crowd came alive, cheering as they led him through to booking. He was headed to the same jail he put people in during his corrupt years on the bench. The dreadful look on his face was most likely from the fear of what would happen to him on the other side.

The police paraded business owners, doctors, police officers, and many other influential members of the community in front of the crowd on their way to booking. Their secret lives were now busted wide open for everyone to see. They also walked the women who enabled these men who physically abused the girls. Some of them may have been victims, too. It was finally over, and the healing would begin for these young women.

It was a wrap on the rehab center. Brian was finishing up the last piece, and I would continue my work on Lexi's story for the magazine.

Lexi. I remember thinking that she needed to know. I needed to tell her it was over for those girls. I texted her to ensure she was home and told her I would stop by if she wasn't busy.

She texted back, *I'm here, come on.*

I walked up to the door and knocked. Lou opened the door.

"Hi, Sammie." She quickly hugged me.

"Hi, Lou, how are you?" I asked.

"I'm good. I'm going to GED classes," she said with the biggest smile on her face.

"Good for you, Lou. I'm proud of you, sister."

"Thank you."

She took my hand and led me into the kitchen, where Lexi was working on homework.

Lexi looked up at me and said, "Hi, Sammie."

"Hey you, are you sure you're not busy?" I asked.

"Nah, you're good, just doing some homework," she said as she closed the laptop.

"I'm so proud of you, Lexi," I said.

"Aww, thanks, and thank you for believing in me."

"You're welcome." I smiled at her. "So, do you have a few minutes? I have some news for you."

"Of course, have a seat," she said as she cleared a spot off the table. "I'm sorry, I have papers everywhere."

"You're fine, no worries."

I sat down. "I don't want to take too much of your time, but I wanted to stop by and let you know I just left the downtown precinct. Several arrests were made at the rehab center, including a judge, lawyers, doctors, and the couple managing it.

Lexi looked at me. "They arrested all of them?"

"Yes, all of them. That's why it took longer than we wanted it to, but they needed to take all of them down at the same time."

"Oh my gosh, that is the best news," she said.

I saw the tears and took her hand.

"What about all the girls?" she asked.

"They have counselors, doctors, and a lot of volunteers who are there assessing their needs. They're working with other facilities to get everyone where their healing can begin."

Lexi silently cried.

"It's over, Lexi. No one else will have to go there," I said.

Lou walked in, and she saw the tears running down Lexi's cheeks. "What's wrong?"

"She's okay, Lou. She's just letting some stuff out."

Lou walked up behind her and rubbed her back.

Lexi said, "They closed it, Lou, and arrested all the bad guys."

"What do you mean?" Lou asked.

Lexi looked at me, and I said, "She means the rehab and group homes have been closed. The people responsible for all the bad stuff are going to jail."

Lou jumped up and down, ran over to me, and gave me the biggest bear hug ever from behind. I let go of Lexi's hand as Lou squeezed the breath out of me.

"Lou, let go of her. You're squeezing too hard," Lexi said.

Lou released me and stepped back. I took a breath.

"I'm sorry, Sammie, I'm just happy it's over," Lou said.

"I know, you're good," I said.

Lou took her phone out of her pocket. She quickly went back to her room and we heard her say, "Guess what, Katy?" Then she closed her door.

Lexi shook her head. "She's going to call everyone she knows."

I laughed. "How about you? How do you feel?" I asked.

"So many things. I don't know if I can put it all into words right now."

"I can only imagine," I said.

We talked for a few more minutes, and I said my goodbyes and headed home.

When I saw how well the girls were doing, it made me happy. They both deserved the best life.

Lou was so sweet, but she was like a bull in a china store when she got excited. She was brilliant and exceeded the educational goals that were set by her and her team. Because she was so young when she went to the girl's home, she struggled with social skills and understanding boundaries. Lou worked with some of the best in the field regarding doctors and therapists. I knew she was going to rock life because she had a fantastic vibe.

Lexi was far more reserved but came out of her shell with her friends. She was driven and had accomplished so much since I met her a few months earlier. She wanted to get an education that would allow her to help others. Even with all she had been through, she refused to see herself as a victim;

she was determined to overcome her physical injuries and the emotional and mental ones as well.

She reminded me of someone I used to know.

†

When I got home, I grabbed an ice-cold bottle of my favorite beer and headed to check my emails. I made it to the couch when the doorbell rang. *UGH!* I looked at the clock; it was 5:30. I wasn't expecting anyone.

A vaguely familiar face was smiling at me when I opened the door.

When I didn't respond, she frowned and said, "You forgot me, haven't ya?"

"I'm sorry. Can I help you with something?" I wasn't sure I wanted her to answer.

"Oh, for the love of Christ, child, I'm your Aunt Marla."

My mother's sister, whom I hadn't spoken to since my grandpa's death. I briefly recalled her staring at me at the funeral. She looked so old and broken. Nothing like the cigarette-toting loudmouth drunk.

"The ladies at Daddy's church said you are here writing something for some fancy magazine." Marla paused and looked around, out of breath as she leaned against the porch railing.

"The lady three houses down from us...." She struggled with a breath, cleared her throat, and began again, "...said that a writer was staying in her sister's house, so I just put two and two together." She smiled at me with a grin that made me feel a little ill.

At that awkward moment I invited her to sit on a porch chair. As she sat down, she said, "Boy, it's hot as hell today."

I wasn't about to invite that woman into the house. Maybe the heat would keep her from overstaying her welcome. Bella lay down by my feet and didn't take her eyes off Marla.

She started talking about life, hers mostly, with a tone that got all over me.

"Me and your uncle live in the same shitty old house down from that old mill..." As she paused again, she started coughing.

I thought of that mill and remembered the odor that used to come from it.

She continued, "Well, they tore the mill down after old man Milberg died. After that, the neighborhood went to hell, and all those people lost their jobs. Now the blacks have moved in and taken over the neighborhood," she rambled on.

It was all coming back to me, the reasons that woman disgusted me.

"One of these days, the walls are going to fall in on me when that damn train goes by," she grumbled. "Fred is the same old bastard he always was, constantly complaining about something. He is a crippled old man who sits in his chair, day in and day out, barking out orders...." She started coughing again.

It seemed the years of smoking had caught up with her.

"Can I get you water?" I asked. She nodded.

As I walked through the house to the kitchen, I contemplated how to end this misery. I handed her the water when I returned to the deck.

27

"Oh, thank you, dear. Your dog looks at me like she wants a piece of me."

"Nah, she doesn't bite."

"Oh, that's good."

Her tone was broken; she was pitiful, but I lacked empathy for that woman. I'd never forget the way she stood back and watched the things my mother did. She finally caught a breath and continued her rant about how crappy her life was and how her kids were worthless.

"Your cousin Julie got married, and she had some kids. She let herself go and lays around in the same clothes all day. She got fat from all her food, and her house is nasty. Well, that husband of hers got tired of it and got caught with the blacksmith's daughter." She shook her head and then said, "He took the kids and married that girl in no time. They moved away. Now your cousin is shacked up with some bum doing nothing with her life, and I don't get to see my grandkids."

She attempted to make a sad face, but her coldness was too visible to have made it believable.

She looked around and said, "You've done good, kid, doing your writing for that fancy magazine. Some people at the restaurant were talking about that book you wrote about that lost girl. They said it was really good, but you know I ain't good at reading. They also said that you must have lots of money with that book and all." She paused for a second and then said, "You know, most people are shocked. They didn't think you'd make it, you know, because of how things were with your ma."

They didn't think I'd make it. What the hell? I didn't respond. I had nothing to say to this woman. The awkward quiet was almost too much.

"So, Sammie, is it true what those people say?"

"I don't know what you're talking about. Who are they?" I asked in an aggravated tone. I braced myself for what would come out of her mouth next.

"Well, someone heard the lady at church saying that you're gonna go to hell because of being queer," she said in a near whisper. "And they say—"

I interrupted her. "Look, I don't want to have this conversation with you."

With a tone of desperation, she said, "Your ma, she said you hated us." She hesitated and continued, "We knew your ma wasn't good to you. But what were we s'pose to do?" she hissed. "We couldn't feed you, too, and you know Ma and Daddy could've..."

I put my hand up, and I stood. This was where it would end. I wasn't going to allow her to bash my deceased grandparents.

"That's enough, and I do not hate you. I don't think of you, and frankly, I have no desire to know you." I walked toward the front door.

As I put my hand on the knob to go inside, I turned to her and said, "You can leave now." I opened the door. "Come on, Bella."

Bella ran inside.

"You don't have to be rude, for Christ's sake," she said as she stood up. She paused, and then asked, "You s'pose you could help an old woman out?"

I walked into the house, closed the door, and locked it. That woman nauseated me, and she would never change. I watched her hobble to her car; she was a pathetic person.

I sat on the couch and pictured Marla watching my mother hurt me. Her visit elicited memories that rushed through my head.

I'd never understand how adults can know that someone is brutalizing a child and do absolutely nothing to stop it. It pissed me off on so many levels, not just because of the things that had happened to me. It was not uncommon for people to turn their backs, especially on a family member.

The thoughts were the first I'd had in so many years. A big part of me hoped that my overactive imagination created those memories. I'd shove them into a place where I felt they couldn't haunt me, and I wanted to leave them where they belonged.

In the past.

Over the years, different counselors and other people tried to pry them out of me. They would tell me to write down those memories. It might have helped me dispose of them, but that would have made them real...I hadn't wanted that.

A therapist mentioned EMDR therapy to me once during my first visit. I didn't know that woman, and her description of it all sounded scary. She said she would have me recall a memory subconsciously and somehow help me change how I processed the memory. I never went back to her. It all seemed a little too experimental, and she appeared a bit too excited to dissect my brain metaphorically.

I decided therapy wasn't for me. I'd survived many things and made a life for myself. No one could take it away from me. I told myself the memories could fuck off. Writing them down was just a waste of time.

But I did see that I had closed myself off to people who tried to get close to me. It was never intentional, and I didn't know how to stop it. It just happened. I focused on my career, starting with my education, and didn't date for a long time. It was easier to concentrate on projects and assignments—especially after a couple of failed relationships. It wouldn't matter to me until the day I found that the things I thought I could simply tuck away and forget were what was holding me back from living the life I always wanted. I thought it was too late, and fear kept me from facing them.

Lexi and Lou were strong and fearless. They opened my eyes to another world where being brave didn't mean tucking it away and just pushing through. They'd push through too, but they did it while facing their fears and processing their memories. It inspired me to do the same. I wanted to be free of the thoughts that held me back. I was in Wisconsin, surrounded by all those doors I feared opening.

When I met Lexi and she shared her story with me, she talked about how alone she felt and how there was no one to help her. Left to feel unlovable and unwanted, she had little hope that she would ever get out. It reminded me of the way I felt as a child on the farm with my mother. The visit from my mother's sister validated the memories swirling around in my mind. Some of them were the ones that led to the peak of my mother's abuse. The flashbacks would force me to confront the things I'd been afraid to face. I began a journey of dissecting my recollections and writing them down. Visits to the places from where the memories came were rough. All I could do was navigate through the flashbacks while articulating them through each stroke of the keys.

That was where the healing began.

CHAPTER THREE

The Farm

October 2015

Memories...

Some people cherished them and may even consider them priceless heart treasures. Hold on tight to them, they said. It would be all that was left someday. People lined their walls with them in matching frames, with identical smiles and freckled-covered faces. Families captured and framed vacations, special events and the first day of school. Pictures of birthdays, big smiles and gifts, holidays, and those times with friends filled albums that sat on the shelf and gathered years of dust.

These treasures didn't exist in the house at the farm, not one picture on the wall or photo album on a shelf. There was just the act of remembering life's moments, the ones that play back through your mind like an old 8mm home movie. The lens of my inner child recalled incidents as if I was there watching my younger self endure them again. They became the voices in my head that would remind me of how unloved I felt. It left a void filled with sadness for the times I missed and could never experience.

I looked for a way to dismiss them forever, so my thoughts would never return to the days with all the pain.

That was what I wanted.

Those memories could've defined me as my life emerged from them. There were times I felt like they were demons that shadowed me through life. I never wanted them to become a representation of darkness or a heaviness I carried. Not wanting the past to become the baggage that followed behind me.

But it did...

When I took the assignment in Milwaukee, I was thirty-nine years old and intensely feared love and intimacy. Love was something I couldn't see in my future. It was a fairy tale I didn't believe in. The people I liked the most were the ones I pushed away the furthest. It was easiest that way.

For years, I thought the things that happened on the farm were because there was something wrong with me. That must've been why no one cared about what happened there. I doubted my memories because, if it was that bad, why did my family not help me?

There were so many thoughts that swirled around in my head for days after the visit. I knew what I needed to do, but I wasn't sure where to begin.

†

The blaring alarm on my phone startled me, and I sat up quickly. Sleep didn't come easy when my mind wouldn't shut off. I grabbed my clothes and rushed to the shower.

I needed a lot of caffeine that morning.

Zoë, my best friend, was flying in from New Mexico that day, and her timing was perfect. Having her in Wisconsin with me was exactly what I needed!

I made it to the airport with a few minutes to spare. While I waited for Zoë, my friend in town called to let me know she was able to get permission from the bank for me to go on my parent's property, the farm where I grew up. I'd swing by the bank later to get the keys from her.

I saw Zoë emerging from the crowd of people. Her short blonde hair was perfectly styled. She looked up and saw me, and we both looked like dorks with our cheesy smiles. Then, in Zoë style, she ran toward me as dramatically as possible, swooped me up, and twirled me around.

"Oh, my God, I am so glad to see you." She squeezed me tight.

"Zoë put me down. You are so crazy!" I laughed.

"And that is why you love me." She put me down and smiled at me. Her beautiful blue eyes were always captivating.

"That is exactly why I love you." I winked at her.

Zoë grabbed my hand. "I'm starving. Can we stop by the brewery with the badass burgers?"

"Yes, of course, we can," I replied.

Zoë had this energy that drew me in and made me happy. Zoë was always playful, a free spirit with a laugh that was contagious. I trusted her more than I had ever trusted anyone. After all the years and the things we had been through, Zoë had never walked away, even when she probably should have. We had met in New Mexico through some mutual friends.

As much as I loved her, I struggled with being comfortable, with becoming too close. I was terrified of catching feelings for her. There was no way I could give Zoë the love she deserved. She would try to make me feel safe, and she never pushed, but the walls were tall, and the layers thick. It seemed wrong not to give her what she needed. She showed me so much compassion and patience. Letting her go was what I felt was best. But she didn't feel the same. We became the best of friends. She always had my back and believed in me more than I did myself.

†

Zoë wanted to go to the beach after we finished lunch. We went by the house to grab hoodies and blankets. We stopped by a liquor store and then headed to the beach. With a cooler in hand, we walked barefoot until we found a place to settle in for conversation and a glass of wine. Zoë got the blanket spread out while I prepared our drinks.

She sat on the blanket. "Fuck, I love this beach."

"Yeah, me too."

36

I sat next to her, and she covered our legs with the blanket.

"Thank you," I said.

"No, thank you."

"I have missed you, Zoë."

"Aww... I've missed you too."

It wasn't the words as much as how she looked at me adoringly that made my heart flutter. But I'd look away every time because of the way it made me feel. It scared me. I stared off at the lake. The sunset was looming behind us while the sound of the waves crashing onto the shore whispered into the air.

"I don't know of any other place that is so peaceful," I said.

"It helps when you are with a badass friend!" Zoë said.

"The baddest ever!" I said.

I winked at her, and we laughed.

We sipped our wine and caught up on everything that had been happening in our lives since we spoke last.

"So, you won't believe who showed up at my place the other night," I said.

"The woman of your dreams?" A joke, it seemed, but the disapproving look on her face indicated that such a scenario wouldn't make Zoë happy.

"Shut up." I playfully shoved her, and we both laughed.

"Who had the nerve to show up at your door uninvited?"

"My mother's sister, Marla."

"What the fuck? Have you seen her since your grandpa's funeral?"

"No, and it was so awkward. That woman is foul."

"Oh, I remember. She glared at me the whole time at your grandpa's funeral. But why did she show up now?" she asked.

I shrugged my shoulders. "Money and sympathy, but she'll get neither from me." I sipped my wine. "I never thought that woman would ever acknowledge the monster that existed in my mother."

"How fucking weird."

"Right? She made the same old excuses and tried to blame my grandparents."

"Damn, I'm sorry, Sam."

"It's all good.... I can't keep running from it, Zoë. I want to go to the farm."

"Really?" she asked.

"I don't know, but something makes me feel like I need to go."

"Good for you, Sam. I'm proud of you," she said.

"Will you go with me to the farm?"

"Of course I will."

†

A few days later, we headed to the farm where I grew up. The images of that place haunted my thoughts for a long time. I felt like I needed to confront them to overcome the impact they had on my life. Zoë insisted on driving, so I tossed her the keys to my rental car. Bella jumped into the back seat. She was always down for a ride.

"Hey, so who owns the farm now?" Zoë asked.

"The bank," I said.

"Oh really? Why is that?"

"My understanding is that my mother sold it after my father died. A girl I went to school with and her husband bought it. She had dreams of opening a training center for kids someday."

"What happened?" Zoë asked.

"She was driving home from her parents when she got hit head-on by a drunk driver, killing her and her daughter. Her husband left the area with their son and let the bank foreclose on the property."

"Oh, wow," Zoë said.

We arrived at the old property in Fredonia. I was surprised to see the buildings standing, the pastures still fenced in, and the gate shut. The pastures didn't look the same as I remembered.

"Wow, it looks so different," I said.

We got out of the car.

"Come on, Bella." She jumped out of the car and followed me.

"I ain't gonna lie. It's creepy," Zoë said.

"Agreed. Let's get this over with." I walked toward the gate.

I stopped and looked at the place that used to represent hell for me. The buildings looked small now, and the driveway used to seem so long. I recalled seeing my grandfather's car pull in and running out to greet him. I remembered the happiness I felt when he used to come to pick me up to see Grandma. When I was a kid, it seemed so big when I wandered around the property alone.

I started pushing on the gate.

"So, are we about to trespass on the land of horrors?"

"No, Zoë, you can relax. My friend's sister works at the bank that foreclosed on the property, and she got permission for me to be here," I said. I pushed on the gate again.

"Need some help there, Wonder Woman?" Zoë asked.

I pushed again with all I had, and finally, it opened enough for us to get through.

"It is like a fucking jungle," Zoë said.

She parted the overgrown grass and stepped carefully, fussing all the way. "Damn, I should have worn different shoes. They're going to get fucked up here."

I laughed. "When did you become such a girly girl?"

"It's the shoes, Sammie. They're my favorites." She laughed.

As we walked around the property, Bella ran ahead checking everything out.

I walked to one of the small barns and stopped in the doorway as I looked around. Zoë came up behind me.

"Did they just leave all this stuff behind?" she asked.

"I don't know. There sure is a lot of junk, though,"

I looked around in disbelief, so much stuff everywhere. There were old toolboxes filled with small tools and odds and ends. My father was a bit of a hoarder, but I didn't remember the stuff being there when he left—maybe it was stored in another building I never entered. There were many things with locks on them around the farm.

"Ugh, cobwebs, I hate cobwebs," Zoë said.

She jumped back, swatting at something.

I laughed.

"You okay?" I asked.

"Yes, I'll be fine."

"It's so crazy how different this looks," I said.

I pointed up and said to Zoë, "I used to climb into that tiny loft. I felt so high off the ground."

"Creepy," she said. She looked up at the loft. "What did they keep in this barn?"

"When I was a kid, this was where they kept the pigs," I said.

I turned around to walk away, and I saw the old waterspout poking out from all the weeds that had grown around it, the old rusty lock still on it. I used to drink water right out of the spout when my mother locked me out of the house. One day I went to the waterspout and found she'd locked it, so I couldn't get water out of it anymore.

We walked to the large barn that used to house the cattle—the door was open. I stepped inside, and the other end of the large gate swung open and then slammed shut.

"What the hell was that?" Zoë asked.

"Why are you so jumpy?"

"Because these buildings are like something out of a horror movie."

"Yeah, they are," I said.

Bella came running into the barn. "Hey, girl."

"Who are you talking to?"

"Bella, go protect Zoë. She's scared," I said.

"You hush, Sammie," she replied playfully.

I looked in the feed room. There were still grain barrels sitting in the same place. I used to hide behind those barrels when my mother was in a drunken rage. She would never look there because she was afraid of mice. Suddenly I remembered Mother walking back and forth through the barn, yelling my name. I ran there to hide because I knew it wouldn't be good if she found me. I hid until I didn't hear her anymore, and I hurried to a more comfortable hiding place.

"You okay, Sammie?"

"Ah yeah, I'm good."

"Memory?"

"Yeah," I said.

Zoë walked up behind me to embrace me. I jumped and pulled away. I just looked at her.

The shock on her face made me feel bad. "I'm sorry, Zoë."

"No, I'm sorry, I didn't mean to...."

"You didn't do anything wrong. It's just this place." I hugged her and said, "I'm so grateful you are here with me." I kissed her on the cheek, then took her hand as we walked around the barn.

The stall on the end was where Tug had stayed, a retired racehorse that came to the farm to live out the rest of his life. A friend of my father's brought him to the farm a couple of years before I left for good. I spent a lot of time brushing him and hanging out with him. I stared into the stall, replaying the day I found him lying still. He didn't get up when I opened his door and didn't move. The vet said he just died in his sleep, with no pain. It was one of the saddest days of my life.

When I turned around, Zoë was looking at the ladder that went up to the hayloft.

"Where does this go?"

I climbed the ladder. "You want to see?"

"Fuck no, Sam, that doesn't look safe."

"It's fine." I reached the top and stood near the edge. "My mother was too afraid to climb the ladder, so I would come up here to write."

I looked around. The window I used to sit under was busted out. There was old hay stacked in one corner. The space seemed so much bigger when I was a kid. I spent a lot of time there dreaming of a future I was told I'd never have. My safe space to be who I wanted to be. I walked to the edge of the hayloft and looked down at Zoë.

"Please, just come down here. You're freaking me out."

Bella started barking as she looked at me.

"See, even Bella thinks you need to come down."

As I climbed down the ladder, Zoë was at the bottom, freaking out.

I stepped on the third rung from the bottom. I heard a crack as it broke, and I fell backward, landing ass-first. All I could do was laugh as Zoë rushed over to ensure I hadn't damaged anything.

"You okay? And why are you laughing?" She tilted her head quizzically.

"Yes, I'm fine, and I don't know why I'm laughing. It just happens."

Bella ran over to make sure I was okay.

Zoë held her hands out to help me up. I grabbed them as she pulled me up and straight into a hug.

"You're so crazy," she said.

I turned around. "How dirty is my ass?"

"It isn't bad." She laughed.

I brushed the dust off the back of my pants. "What are you laughing about?"

"You're so adorable," she said.

Adorable? Did she say adorable? I turned around and Zoë had a smirk on her face and was looking at my ass.

"What's with the ogling?"

"Ogling?"

"Staring at my ass?"

"Well...." Zoë giggled.

Is she blushing? Surely not.

"Shut it! Let's get out of here," I said.

"Yes, I like that idea," she said.

We walked out of the barn and headed toward the house. I hesitated when I got to the door. I looked at Zoë and took a deep breath.

When I opened the door, I couldn't believe what I saw. It was as if time had stood still, and all my mother's stuff remained in the house, in the same place she had left it all those years ago. I walked over to the kitchen sink and looked out the window. The apple trees were no longer there, and the paddocks were gone.

I remembered doing dishes, repeatedly, in hot bleach water at that window for hours. I would daydream while doing the dishes and imagine myself in a different place with another mother. The refrigerator wasn't in the same place, but I could still picture the old one.

I was deep in thought when Zoë spoke, and it startled me. "Damn it. I'm sorry, Sammie. I didn't mean to scare you... again."

"It's okay. I was just deep in thought. I'm ready. Let's get out of this house."

"Yes, please!" she said.

We walked behind the house.

During the times that Mother wasn't drinking, we'd play catch in the yard. In the winter, I'd slide down the hill that was behind the house. There was an old dog pen that was barely standing at the bottom of the hill. Chicken coops were hardly visible through the overgrown landscape.

We continued to walk around the property when I saw something sticking out of the ground.

"Oh, my God!" I pulled the toy out of the ground. "This was my truck and horse trailer that my Uncle Bill gave me for Christmas one year. It had a horse that went with it, too." I wiped the dirt off as I looked it over. "I got this the year we found out Grandma had cancer."

Looking around as I sat the old dirty object down, a memory flashed through my mind of the night Mother gathered all my toys and told me I would never see them again.

"What are you thinking about, Sammie?"

"On New Year's Day, Mother got drunk and tripped over one of my toys. It pissed her off, so she took all the toys I'd received that year and got rid of them. She must have buried them here," I said.

"Wow, she was something else. Who does that?"

I shrugged my shoulders. "A raging alcoholic who drank a lot of whiskey." I stared off for a moment as I replayed memories in my mind. "She was never mother of the year material, but when she went off the whiskey, she was different." I looked at Zoë. "It seemed she despised the sight of me when she drank. It didn't take much to make her mad enough to want to beat my ass."

"It sounds like your mother had some serious issues," Zoë said.

"Yeah, as a kid, I couldn't sort it out in my mind. I thought there was something wrong with me. But it was my mother that had the problem. I was just dealt a terrible hand and did the best I could to survive and get out as soon as I could. It made me who I am." I looked at Zoë. "You know what I mean?"

"Yeah, I get it. It's okay to need to heal, too," she said.

"I know it is." I grabbed her hand. "You ready to get out of here?"

"Yes, ma'am!"

I whistled for Bella, and she came running.

As we drove away, I refused to look back. That was my past, and there would never be a reason to return.

A few years later, the developers would demolish it all to make way for commercial lots.

The land of horrors. Forever gone.

The memories, although somewhat faded, would always remain.

CHAPTER FOUR

Mother

Mother hated me. I saw it in her eyes every time she looked at me.

As I grew older, there were times I hated her, too, and most of the time, I avoided eye contact.

She often threatened me with a life behind the tall fence, inside a brick building that didn't have any windows—a place filled with bad kids, like me, the unlovable ones, according to my mother. I was never sure what made me inadequate or unlovable. I was just born that way.

Mother would be gone for days when she got on a drunken binge. Then she would come home and spend hours yelling at me, calling me names, and making me beg her not to take me to that place. Sometimes I just wanted to tell her to take me there because anything had to be better than staying with my mother. I knew better than to speak because it would make it worse. But I had lots of thoughts about things I would do if only I were brave.

I preferred it when she whipped me. It was faster. It hurt for a while, and then it was gone. I didn't have to listen to her tell me how worthless I was and how no one would ever love me. She would spend hours tormenting me with words, laughing at me if I cried, and calling me names I had never heard before.

There were many thoughts I never spoke about, and I saved them for the diary my grandparents gave me for my twelfth birthday.

†

My birthday was memorable in more than one way. At the lunch table, Ally, a school acquaintance, talked about her birthday. Her family celebrated her for a week, with favorite meals and a game night. She always had a big party with lots of friends. I never attended her parties but heard they were fun.

There was no celebrating me or my birth on the farm. Most years, there was no acknowledgment, and the day was just a typical one with Mother. I woke up shortly after midnight to a loud noise. I tried to open my eyes, but the brightness of the light blinded me.

"Get up," I heard Mother say. She stood in the doorway of my room. My stomach felt sick when I smelled the whiskey in the air. Mother was drunk.

"Why?" I asked without thinking.

She grabbed me by my nightgown and started dragging me to the truck. "What did I do?" I desperately asked.

"Shut the fuck up and get in the back."

Mother peeled out of the driveway and took off so fast, I was scared we would crash. I closed my eyes and prayed. The next thing I knew, Mother slammed on the brakes, and I hit the back of her seat hard.

When the truck stopped, I looked out the window and saw that we were in front of that place, the building with tall fences. I didn't know why we were there. Mother swung open the door, and I drew back in fear. Trying to get away from her only made her angrier; she grabbed my hair and pulled me out of the truck.

"On your knees, it's time you start begging."

"No, please, I didn't do..." Before I could say anymore, she slapped me across my face so hard it knocked me back.

"Yes, you did, you ran your mouth to one of your stupid little friends, and I got questioned by someone today. I told you not to talk about anything that happens here to anyone. On your damn knees," she said. She grabbed me by my hair and slammed me back on my knees. The sting on my face was nothing compared to the gravel digging into my skin. The pain was almost unbearable, but I knew better than to say anything. It would only get worse.

"If they come to take you, they will put your ass in foster care. Ain't no one going to take you in. Now beg before I go in there and tell them you are a lying thief," she screamed.

I tried to ignore the pain in my knees as my mother laughed at me and made fun of the way I looked while I begged. She ridiculed me as she made me recite, "Please, I beg you, don't make me go where the bad kids go. I know I'm a bad kid."

This went on for a while before she came over and slapped me upside my head and yelled, "Now pray, you worthless brat."

"Please, God, make me a good kid so I don't have to go to that place. If you only make me good, I'll do everything."

She laughed at me as she guzzled her beer. It went on for what seemed like hours. I couldn't do it anymore. I was so tired and could feel my body start to slump as the heaviness took over.

"Oh fuck no, you ain't done yet." She slapped me across my face.

I was so tired. My body felt heavy and ached, and I didn't even know what I did besides exist. There was never any conversation with anyone about home or about what went on there. I would have been too embarrassed to tell my friends, anyway. Silent was how I existed on the farm.

"Can't hear you!" she yelled.

"Please, God, make me a good kid...." It was so hard to stay in that position. My body trembled as my knees screamed with pain. My head burned from where she pulled the hair out of my head. I felt the welts on my face from her repeatedly slapping me. I smelled like beer from her spilling it on me. She blew her smoke in my face, and if I turned away, she hit me and grabbed my face so she could blow it again. She knew I hated cigarette smoke, so she did it.

I fell over, and Mother grabbed my hair again, but this time it was to drag me back to the truck because the sun had begun to come up. I curled up in a ball, fell asleep, and heard the door open again. We were home.

"Come on, brat, you need to get your ass dressed for school."

I got out of the truck, could barely stand from exhaustion, and my body hurt badly. Walking was painful because my knees hurt so much. Mother shoved me into the house and laughed as I hit the floor.

"Get up now. I hope you learned not to run your fucking mouth again."

As quickly as possible, I went to my room and found the clothes I had set out for school—my favorite outfit. I had waited for over a week to wear it. In my closet hung only four outfits for school. Mother let me put them in the laundry one day a month. I quickly put my clothes on so I could eat some breakfast. It smelled so good. Breakfast only happened on the days Father was home, and I could smell the bacon he had cooked. He was making scrambled eggs, too; the smell of the food made my stomach jump.

I sat down, and Mother said, "Oh no, no breakfast for you. You took too goddamn long to get dressed." Then she laughed as she took a bite of her bacon.

Father turned around from the stove and said, "For Christ's sakes, Connie, let that child eat. I don't know why you always have to be a bitch."

"Fuck you, dumbass," she said as she launched a bottle at him, shattering it as it hit the back of his head.

Father grabbed his head, "Jesus Christ, Connie. You are a crazy bitch." He walked away, blood running down his hand as he held his head.

She looked at me. "You get the fuck out of here and get to your bus stop. I best not hear of you falling asleep in school."

†

School sucked. I was so tired that I could barely stay awake but couldn't draw attention to myself. If they called Mother, my life would be hours of hell. I couldn't wait until lunch. The gnawing feeling in my stomach was intense. While Ally talked about her upcoming birthday, I was stuffing my face with the pizza they served for lunch. The girls talked about it being the worse they ever had, but I liked it, which might be because it was the only pizza I got. We also had a piece of carrot cake. To be honest, I didn't really like it, but I ate it anyway.

When I got home, Father was gone, and Mother was not home either. I was relieved that she wasn't there. Even though keeping my eyes open was difficult, I did my chores and wanted nothing more than to take a bath. But I was only allowed a shower once a week. Mother turned off the hot water and locked the closet with the water heater. My mother only allowed hot water for dishes. My showers were cold. I went to bed early, my body ached, and my knees throbbed from the lingering pain. I was asleep as soon as I lay down and closed my eyes.

That's what I remember about my twelfth birthday.

†

It was a couple of weeks after my birthday when Mother showed up at home with pizza and a cake.

"Sammie, I got us some pizza."

"Pizza? Really, Mother?" I asked.

"Well, that is what I said, ain't it?"

I couldn't believe it. Mother never got pizza.

"I got some cake, too. I know it was your birthday a couple of weeks ago, and I didn't even tell you happy birthday." She walked over and handed me a plate.

"Let's have some pizza and cake. Then I have a surprise for you."

"A surprise, Mother?" I asked.

"Yes, a surprise."

I didn't know how to act. Mother didn't bring surprises.

We ate, and Mother even let me have two pieces of cake. Then we went outside, and Mother took me to the barn. We walked into the feed room, and there was the fluffiest, black-and-white puppy. She ran right up to me as I kneeled. She climbed into my lap and kissed my face.

"What do you think, Sammie?" she asked.

"She is all mine?" I asked.

"Well, yeah."

"Oh, thank you, Mother. I love her. I'll take good care of her, I promise."

†

I often dreamt of a different life with a mother who loved me and a father that was there. There was no doubt that Grandpa and Grandma loved me, but I felt alone and scared when I was at the farm. Never was what happened on the farm ever mentioned, because my mother said I'd never get to see them again. She would make sure of it. They didn't know how often I stayed home alone. They never knew. Even though I got scared sometimes, I would rather be home alone than with her. I'd rather be anywhere but on the farm with Mother. She treated the animals better than me, and I was sure she liked them more.

When her friends came over, she would tell me before they got there, "I tell you now, if you make one peep or I see you, you're going to regret it."

I avoided eye contact with my mother most of the time.

"We understand each other?" she asked.

I nodded.

Being around a bunch of drunks wasn't what I wanted, anyway. They were loud and someone was always fighting. I was happy to go to my hiding place and avoid all of them. Waiting until they were busy doing their thing, I snuck out the back door and headed toward the barn. I looked back to ensure Mother didn't see me entering the barn. It wasn't likely that she would come looking, but I instinctively looked back.

Once in the barn, I climbed the wobbly ladder to the hayloft. It was the only way up, and Mother would never go there. She was afraid of heights and already told my father, "You are dumb if you think I'm getting up there."

I used her fears to secure a hiding place for myself. I kept my spiral notebooks, pencils, erasers, and my diary behind a bale of hay in the hayloft—just in case someone else came up there and asked Mother about them. If she found out they were there, she would have burned them in the barrel.

†

I didn't know how she got to my notebooks, but she had them in her hand and was heading to the burn barrel. She threw the first notebook into the barrel.

"Please, Mother, don't.... please don't burn them."

That only pissed her off more. She turned to look at me. "I told you before, you're too dumb to be writing any goddamn stories." Then she threw the next one in the barrel; as the flames shot up in the air, she cackled, "Who do you think is going to read your stupid stories?"

She threw the last notebook into the fire, and I went to my knees as I cried. As she walked by me, she said, "Maybe I need to give you something to cry about?"

I felt a brutal hit to the side of my head. I tried not to react, but it hurt, and I cried harder.

"Weak. My mother has made you weak." She kicked me in the middle of the back, and I fell face-first into the ground. "Fucking crybaby," she said as she walked away.

The physical pain didn't compare to the feeling in my heart because she'd destroyed something very special to me for no reason. It made me so sad. I didn't understand why she hated me and wanted to take anything I cared about away from me.

†

Sometimes we went to my father's parent's house for Sunday dinner. I didn't know them well and rarely saw them. They didn't allow drinking at their farm. My parents acted differently around them.

"So, Sammie won an essay contest last week," my father said.

"Is that right?" my grandfather asked.

"I told her she was a talented writer," my mother said. "If she would only do her schoolwork, she could go somewhere."

"Good job on your essay, Sammie," Grandma said.

"Thank you," I quietly replied.

"Sammie, you need to be doing your schoolwork," Grandpa said.

"Yes, sir," I said.

I looked up at my mother, who was smiling from ear to ear.

"She does her homework when she gets done with all of her chores," Father said.

"Maybe the child needs fewer chores, so she has more time for her schoolwork," Grandma said.

They quickly changed the subject. Mother was a different person when she wasn't drinking and around my father's family. She tried to be mother of the year, but I always knew it would be over as soon as we got in the car to go home. Mother and Father would argue all the way home. Then the drinking began, and peace would be lost to toxic chaos and sometimes violent fights.

CHAPTER FIVE

My Grandparents

I have very few memories of my mother before my twelfth birthday. It might've been because I spent a lot of time with my grandparents. We had a special bond. Most of my childhood memories are of my grandparents; the rest weren't worth remembering. When with them, I felt loved, safe, and could be a carefree kid.

My grandparents took me to do a lot of things. My favorite places to go with them was the county fair and the mall. I could still remember my grandmother's laughter as we rode the Tilt-A-Whirl, and Grandpa's enthusiasm when we attended the Demolition Derby at the fair. When we went to the mall, Grandpa and I always went to the little restaurant across from Montgomery Ward's. That was Grandma's favorite store, but Grandpa and I didn't like shopping, so we would sit at the little bar with the milkshake machine behind it, get a shake, and wait until Grandma finished shopping.

Mother would never take me to the mall. I asked her once, and she said, "Oh, hell no, that place is for snobby city folks and them blacks that have moved in."

I knew better than to ask her twice.

†

One weekend I was with my grandparents, and there was an incident with Mother. It happened after my twelfth birthday—when the physical abuse escalated to a new level of violence.

We spent the morning at the mall. When we got home, Grandpa and I played cards while Grandma made cookies and worked on her puzzle. Grandpa's brother stopped by so he went downstairs to talk to him. I heard her truck. As I hid under the table, I informed Grandma, "Mother's here." I hoped I wouldn't have to go with her if she didn't see me.

Mother came stumbling in the door of Grandma's house, a can of Stroh's beer in her hand and Aunt Marla trailing her. She was yelling for me to come out because she wanted me to go with her.

Grandma told her she wouldn't allow her to take me out of the house, and my mother told Grandma to screw off. She asked Aunt Marla where I was, and even though she looked right at me a time or two, she shrugged her shoulders and kept drinking her beer. When Mother didn't stop, Grandma yelled for Grandpa and his brother. They both came up the stairs, and Grandma told them Mother needed to be taken out of the house and driven home.

Mother started yelling and cussing as she nearly hit the floor because she was so drunk. Grandpa motioned to my uncle, and they grabbed her from each side and dragged her outside. She was screaming and cussing at them the whole way. Aunt Marla stood there, staring at me. As I crawled from under the table, she gave me a stone-cold look. Relief came over me as I looked out the window and saw the taillights fading. I turned around and squeezed Grandma as hard as I could. I loved her so much.

†

I remember that night, after Mother left and Grandma tucked me into bed, I overheard Aunt Marla and Grandma talking.

I heard Marla say, "This ain't my fault, Ma. You know I can't stop her from drinking if she wants to."

"You don't discourage it either, and you are right there with her, drinking just as much."

"Well, hell, she ain't gonna listen to me anyhow, Ma."

"She doesn't listen to anyone, but it doesn't mean you need to be out there drinking beside her. You sure as hell don't need to be bringing her back here to terrorize that child."

"Shit, you know there ain't no stopping her from doing that, either. She's gonna do what she wants to do."

I could barely hear Grandma say, "Someone is going to have to protect her if—" I wasn't able to hear the rest of what she said. I dozed off to the sound of their whispering.

†

I remember the following day when I bounced out of bed and ran downstairs to the living room, where my grandma usually sat in her brown rocker chair. Most mornings, I would find her crocheting as she waited on the bread she was baking to finish. We had our routine. My favorite thing to do was to brush her hair. She loved it so much.

But on that morning, she was nowhere to be found. Not in the kitchen, and not in her chair in the living room. I looked all over the house. I started to head upstairs when my grandpa suddenly appeared. I could tell by the look on his face that something was wrong. His hair was uncombed, and his favorite cap was not on his head, as usual. Nothing was normal about the morning. I asked Grandpa where Grandma was, and he told me she wasn't feeling well. I told him I wanted to see her and started up the stairs, but he stopped me and told me she was at the hospital.

"No, she was just fine last night. What happened to her? I want to go to the hospital to see her," I cried.

"I'm afraid you can't go up there yet. The doctors had to put Grandma in a special room to help her. They don't allow children in the unit. Aunt Marla is coming to take you home."

"No, Grandpa. Can I go with you? Please."

I was so afraid I would never see Grandma again.

We found out just days after they admitted Grandma to the hospital that she had cancer. I overheard Grandpa and my aunts saying it was the kind they couldn't cure. I wasn't sure what cancer was, but I knew it sounded terrible. Grandpa told me they were going to do surgery on her stomach that might help make it go away. If everything went well, she could come home.

Every night I hit my knees and prayed for two things. The first was that the doctors would make my grandma better so she could come home. The second was for God to make me a good kid so my mother would like me more. My prayers went unanswered. Grandma didn't come home, and Mother's anger only seemed to grow.

†

Grandma had been in the hospital for several weeks when the next incident with Mother happened. I was out doing my chores and had just finished feeding the animals in the small barn and was about to head to the cattle barn when Mother came out of the house. I looked up and accidentally made eye contact with her.

"What the fuck are you looking at?" she asked.

I quickly looked away, hoping that would be enough to stop her from getting mad.

"Hey, I'm talking to you," she said as she came toward me. "You better look at me when I'm talking to you." I looked at her, and I could feel the tension building in my body.

"Where the fuck do you think you're going?"

"I'm going to the cattle barn to feed them," I said.

"No, you ain't. You can go right back in there and clean those pens." She pointed at the small barn.

"I cleaned the pens this morning." The words slipped past my quivering lips, and my body shuddered as I braced myself for what would come next. Darkness was coming, and I struggled to breathe because I knew the monster was about to come out. I should've stayed silent.

"Who the fuck do you think you are.... talking to me like that?" she asked. She picked something off the ground.

"I'm sorry..."

"Did I ask you to speak to me?" she asked.

I shook my head as I looked at the ground. I could smell the alcohol in the air. She was drunk again. "Does a nobody get to speak without being asked?"

Again, I shook my head no as I looked at the ground. Before I knew it, she was behind me. She grabbed a fist full of hair and started pulling me to the small barn.

"You are a pain in my ass, always having to tell you to do shit right," she said as she continued to drag me by my hair. I felt the burning on my skull from the hair she ripped out of my head. Once in the barn, she shoved me hard into one of the pigs' pens. I lost my balance and fell hands-first into a fresh pile of poop.

Mother laughed and said, "Don't look like that pen has been cleaned to me." She walked out of the barn.

I stood and headed toward the waterspout right outside the barn door. I turned the water on. Mother spun around. "What the fuck do you think you're doing?" she asked.

"Washing my hands," I answered.

"Did I say you could wash your goddamned hands?" she snarled.

I didn't respond.

She came over to me, grabbed my hair, and pulled me back. "I didn't say you can wash your fucking hands." She let go of me and said, "Get back in that barn and clean up that stall now." She started toward the house.

"Mother, please," I pleaded with her.

I turned back toward Mother as she started coming toward me with her hand raised. Before I could react, she swung at me. She made contact with my face and mouth with whatever she had in her hand. The impact was hard, breaking my teeth, splitting my lip and busting my chin open.

A loud shriek came out of me as the pain hit, and blood gushed from my mouth. My father was pulling into the driveway as I ran toward the house, my mother chasing after me. "I didn't mean to do that, Sammie. Come back here." I didn't stop. I just kept running and screaming.

I heard my father say, "Connie, what the fuck have you done?"

"She was back talking to me again," Mother said.

Father drove to the hospital. Mother sat in the back seat with me, repeatedly saying, "Sammie, I didn't mean to hurt you like that. You gotta stop back talking to me. If someone asks you, you tell them you tripped and busted your mouth and chin on the stairs, you hear me?"

Mother did all the talking at the hospital. The doctors and nurses seemed to buy her story, and she was good at pretending she loved me in front of other people. The doctor poked me with a needle and then stitched me up. I closed my eyes tight so that I couldn't see. I thought he would never finish. When he finally did, he told my mother I needed to see a dentist as soon as possible. I had several broken teeth. I'd have to be on a liquid diet for a while.

"There is a lot of damage, and it will take time to heal. No solid food for a while."

That'd be easy. I didn't eat much, anyway.

When we returned home, Mother got the soft blankets out of the closet and a soft pillow. She was going to allow me to sleep on the couch. "Sammie, what do you want to watch on tv tonight?" she asked.

"Mother? I get to pick the show?" I asked.

"That's what I said," she replied.

Mother would quit drinking from time to time. I thought it was because my grandma was making her do it. Other times she would quit for a while after an incident caused me injury. I didn't know if she was afraid of the consequences if someone found out or if she felt guilty. Either way, it was a break from the fear and pain I experienced when she was drunk.

It wasn't often and wouldn't last for long. But when it did happen, there would be a few days when Mother was kinder than normal. We would even go get a burger and sometimes ice cream. There were occasional trips along the shore with a stop at the corner store to get a coke for the road. Mother wasn't an affectionate person, and we didn't talk much. She would turn up the radio, and we just drove and drank our cokes. I was okay with that. I liked the music and enjoyed the ride. I remembered the smell of fire from the many campgrounds we'd pass along our way, and the wind on my face as we drove along the lake with our windows down.

Every time I'd hope it would last because I didn't want it ever to end. But it always did, the minute she took her next first shot of whiskey.

CHAPTER SIX

Cancer

1990

Sadness...emotional pain associated with loss, sorrow, despair, and helplessness.

The hardest thing I had to do as a teenager was watch a horrible disease that had no mercy take my grandma from me. No amount of praying would change the outcome. I would lose her anyway. I prayed many times a day, hoping for a miracle, like the kind they talked about in church. Mother always told me there were no miracles and that God would not hear me. I never really knew what she meant. I just quit praying because nothing changed. Things would only get worse.

I'll never forget the day Grandpa's car pulled into the driveway. I remember quickly going outside to greet him. As soon as he got out of the car, I ran over and hugged him tightly.

It was a Saturday. Grandpa usually came to get me on Sunday mornings to visit Grandma, but I never cared what day it was. I was just happy to see him.

"Grandpa, do I get to go with you today?" I asked.

"Yes, sweetheart. Where's your ma?"

I shrugged my shoulders.

"Is she in the house?"

I shook my head no.

"How long have you been alone?"

I knew answering his questions wouldn't be good for me if Mother found out.

Just the thought of what could happen would make my skin crawl. I shrugged my shoulders again.

I remember the way he looked at me that day—like he was upset with me for not answering his questions. To disappoint him was never my goal, but he couldn't protect me from my mother. I'd wonder often if he knew I couldn't tell him because if I did, the wrath of Mother would be taken out on my skin.

"Well, I assume she isn't here, so let's get some clothes from your room."

"I can go get them, Grandpa," I said.

I felt a rush of panic come over me when I recalled that moment. Mother would've been furious if I had let him in. I ran toward the house and into my room to get the clothes. They were dirty, but all I had, so I stuffed them under my arm and turned around to get back out to...

Grandpa.

Standing in the doorway.

His eyes were wide, and his eyebrows raised as he looked around the room. He was clearly shocked by what he saw...empty space. There was a broken dresser and my pillow and blanket.

"Sammie, where is your bed?"

"I don't have one right now."

There had been no bed for a while, and I doubted there were any plans to get one. I didn't want to tell him it was because I peed the bed. I was embarrassed I did it when I was ten years old. My mother was on a drunken binge and locked me in my room for several days. I wasn't allowed to use the bathroom. She left me with saltine crackers and a big pitcher of water. I lost track of how many days it had been. I accidentally peed on my bed and, on the carpet, despite trying to hold it. Mother was so mad. She threw the bed away, tore out the carpet, and told me I didn't deserve a bed or carpet.

"Why?" he asked. I shrugged my shoulders. I couldn't tell him.

"What goes on here?" He covered his face with his hand and spun around. "Oh my God."

"Sorry, Grandpa."

He turned around and took my hand.

"Oh honey, I'm not mad at you." He hugged me. "You have nothing to be sorry for, Sammie."

When we walked through the kitchen to leave, Grandpa suddenly stopped. "Why are the cupboards locked?" He looked around. "The refrigerator is locked too?"

I remember the way his eyes held sadness. Nothing I could say would make it go away. He crossed over the threshold of my hell. Eyes wide open.

Mother never let my grandparents into the house because she didn't want them to see this. She didn't need their nosey asses in her house. I knew what happened that day would bring a beating for me. It always did.

Grandpa interrupted my thoughts. "Sammie, when was the last time you ate?"

"Last night, Father made some meatloaf and mashed potatoes. He gave me some before he left."

My father was a truck driver, and he was rarely home. When he was there Mother rode his ass and cussed at him constantly. One time, she broke a chair over his head when he told her to take the locks off the cupboards. I heard him tell Mother he wasn't going to come home anymore, that she could start paying the bills. She would threaten him with things I didn't understand. But he always returned, leaving money to pay the bills and buy groceries. My mother would buy a few groceries, and the ones she did were locked up.

When my father came around, we didn't talk much. He never once asked me about the things Mother did. He was more of a stranger than a parent. My father knew what was going on, but he wouldn't do anything because he didn't want her rage turned on him. When Mother got crazy, he turned his back and walked away.

"Are you hungry, Sammie?" Grandpa asked.

I shrugged. "Not really."

I remembered how the hunger pangs felt. A raw feeling in my gut that would increase in intensity at night. I adapted because the pain got less severe with time. It wasn't a good idea to complain about being hungry; it would only get worse.

"Well, let's go get some lunch."

We had lunch at a restaurant that was one of our favorites when I was a kid. Then we drove to my grandparents. Going to my grandparents was always exciting because there I could be a kid. It was a safe place..

I sank into the bathtub, taking in the way the warm bath felt on my achy body. Surrounded by the fluffy bubbles that were layered on the surface of the water. The scent of coconut from the bubble bath would always remind me of their home.

When I walked out to the kitchen, Grandpa was off the phone and asked me to come to sit with him at the table. I remember the look on his face and knowing something serious was going on. I sat down at the table. Grandpa squeezed my hand gently as he held it. "Sammie, I want to talk to you about a few things."

"Okay."

"We'll visit Grandma today, but she is very weak and tired."

"Why is she weak?"

"The cancer that we talked about has spread, and she's sick," he said.

I felt him squeeze my hand.

"But the medicine will improve her so she can come home."

He shook his head as he looked at me. "No, honey, the medicine isn't working anymore."

I felt the first tear hit my chee., "No, Grandpa...don't say that. Why would God do that to us?"

"He needs her with him now."

"NO! Why is he so selfish? I need her with me, Grandpa."

"It's going to be okay, Sammie."

"No, no, it's never going to be okay." I pulled my hand away and laid my head on my arms, resting on the table. I wondered what would become of me, who would protect me. She was the only one besides Grandpa that loved me.

Grandpa tried to comfort me, but I couldn't imagine my life without Grandma. He told me I would need to be brave for Grandma. He said that no matter how much she wanted to stay with us, she couldn't. We had to let her know we would be okay so she could rest in peace.

After a few minutes, Grandpa said, "How about we go visit Grandma? She was asking for you this morning."

"Right now?"

"Yes, Sammie, right now!"

Grandma was asleep when we got to the nursing home.

"Can I lie with her, Grandpa?" I asked.

He nodded and helped me get on the bed. I crawled up as close as possible and snuggled up to her. When she woke up, she looked at me and smiled.

"Hi, Sammie," she whispered.

I recall that moment, and her voice was no longer hers. There was a difference in the way her arms felt around me. The sparkle in her eye...was gone.

I saw the tears rolling down Grandma's face. "Don't cry, Grandma. It's going to be okay."

"Baby, I'm sorry. God has other plans for me and needs me in heaven."

"I know, Grandma. I wish you could stay. I know God needs you now, but I'll miss you."

"Sammie...I'm sorry. I don't have much longer. I can't be here with you, but I will be with you every day." She started coughing. Grandpa handed her a cup of water. She took a moment before continuing. "I know your mother isn't good to you, and I am so sorry she is like that. But honey...you need to know..." she hesitated. "You need to know you are smart and beautiful." I could tell it was hard for her to talk. "We need you to stay strong," she whispered.

"I will, Grandma, I promise."

"Grandpa is going to..." she struggled to speak. "Grandpa and Aunt Sally are going to get you out of your ma's."

He stepped up to the bed. "We have a lawyer helping us. He said it won't be much longer, Sammie. You'll be with me part of the time, and at Aunt Sally's the rest of the time."

Grandma asked me, "Can you stay strong—for me?"

"Yes." The tears ran down my face. "Is it true no one else will ever love me?"

"Listen, Sammie. You will be loved by many. You will do good things. I know you will." She paused. "Baby, I need you to know you can do anything; you are beautiful." She grabbed my hand.

"You cannot let anything, or anyone break you." She looked at me.

I hugged her tight. The cancer had eaten away at her, and when I hugged her, I could feel how small she had become.

"Sammie," she whispered.

I leaned back and looked at her. "Yes, Grandma."

"You must tell the people who come to talk to you the truth. Don't be afraid."

There was an incident where my mother beat me with a belt during a drunken rage. Some people in suits showed up to the school to question me about the marks my gym teacher saw on my legs. I refused to talk to them. I didn't trust them to help me. I assumed that was what Grandma was referring to and I just agreed because I didn't want her to worry.

That was the last time I got to hear her voice, the last time I felt her arms around me, and my heart was broken.

Mother got a call three days after that last visit. I heard my mother asking how long Grandma had left. Then she grabbed the bottle of whiskey she had been sipping on and started heading toward the door.

"Please let me go see her, PLEASE," I screamed as I ran toward her.

"You are fucking sneaking around listening to my conversations?"

She grabbed the belt she hung on a hook in the living room. She came at me quickly and swung the belt at me. It made contact with my face. The burn came fast, but I didn't care.

"Please, Mother, I want to see her."

"That's it." She grabbed me and pushed me toward the couch. "Pants down and lean over the couch. You know you're not supposed to listen to my conversations or talk back. You're doing both, so you get double the swats."

I lowered my pants and leaned over the couch. I lost count of how many times she hit me, but I remember feeling the belt break my skin as she viciously swung it, leaving its mark on every inch from the waist down.

She grabbed me by the hair and got in my face. "Not another word from you." She pushed me back, and I hit the floor hard.

The door slammed shut. I heard the rumble of her truck's engine and the sound of gravel hitting the side of the porch as she spun out of the driveway. Watching as her taillights disappear, I pulled my pants up and hobbled back to the bedroom, my legs and butt were burning and weak. I started a bath so I could sit in it. The cold water felt good on my welts. After getting out of the bath, I applied some ointment on the broken skin on my legs and butt. Then I went to my room, laid back on my bed on the floor, and cried myself to sleep.

†

A week later, I was sitting alone in the back of the room. All the chairs were lined up in perfect rows and faced the casket. The casket was made of oak and had been surrounded by lots of flowers. It was open, but I didn't go near it. I didn't want to see Grandma like that, and Grandpa said I wouldn't have to.

The wallpaper in the back was odd, and the burgundy-colored fancy curtains seemed as old as the man that greeted us when we walked in. All the adults were huddled in small groups, whispering amongst themselves. Grandma kept the family together. Most of the time, it took a lot of fussing to get them to show up. I hated going because the adults always stared at me like I had two heads. There had always been a lot of whispering going on when I was in the room. I never knew what it was all about.

I looked around, and the room was getting more crowded. It was almost time for the funeral to start. I thought about how I would rather be anywhere but here. I hated it when people stared and whispered. The room went quiet when my mother walked in the door with Aunt Marla. I knew as soon as I saw her that something terrible was about to happen.

If only I could disappear.

One of my great aunts walked over and asked me if I was okay. I nodded my head, and she moved on her way. So far, Mother had not spotted me, and she was talking to some man that walked in after her. A few minutes later, I turned around just in time to see my mother looking at me. I accidentally made eye contact with her, and she started coming toward me.

The smell of whiskey made me feel sick and tremble inside. My mother grabbed me and started dragging me toward the casket I had been avoiding. I was fighting with all my strength, holding chairs as I tried to keep her from taking me, but she kept dragging me.

"No, please, I don't want to see her like that."

She grabbed my arm tighter and said, "Too fucking bad, you brat."

Her grip hurt my arm, and I started screaming, "Please stop. You're hurting me."

"Nobody cares. Now stop screaming. You're making a scene, and when we get home, I will deal with you."

They all stood there...staring with their mouths hanging wide open in disbelief. Not one of those adults did a thing to stop it. I never understood how they could stand around and watch her do the things she did without intervening.

My Aunt Sally rushed in from another room. "Connie, let go of that girl now."

"Fuck off, Sally." She continued to drag me toward the casket.

"Mother, please, no, don't do this, please," I screamed.

"You think because all these people are here, you can talk to me like that?"

She tightened her grip on me as she swung around and slapped me across the face. I heard people in the room gasp as her hand made contact. She raised her hand to hit me again when Grandpa and his brother came around the corner.

As they came toward her, she slapped me again and shoved me away hard, and I landed in front of my Aunt Sally. I was quick to cover my head in case she came after me again. Grandpa tried to get her to leave, but she kept cussing at him, so they grabbed her and tried to get her out of the room.

She broke free, started screaming, and pointed her finger at me. "Because of her, I lost my mother a long time ago. That selfish brat took all her time and turned her against me." She looked around at everyone as they stood and watched. "What the fuck ya looking at? Do you pity that ugly, unpleasant child? My mother made her a weak and whiny brat," Mother said.

She came at me again. I ducked and covered my head. Grandpa grabbed her. "That's it, Connie; you're leaving now."

"Oh, fuck you and the rest of you assholes around here. You will learn what that kid is all about and understand why I do what I have to do with her."

A couple of officers walked in and started toward my mother. "Are you fucking kidding me? One of you assholes called the police? We are at my mother's funeral; you can all fuck off."

The police led her from the room. Before they got through the door, she turned around and looked at me. "You wait until you get home. There will be no one to stop me, and you will pay for what you have done, you little bitch."

Those were the last words I heard from my mother's mouth. She would never get the chance to hurt me again. The judge gave them an emergency order to remove me from the house. She went on her way, never looking back. No one ever spoke of her, not around me, anyway. My father just disappeared. Rumor was he shacked up with a much younger woman.

After Grandma's funeral, I went home with Grandpa for a couple of weeks before going to live with Aunt Sally. I remember her being excited about taking me shopping. I'd hear her tell her friends how she always wanted a daughter. But she would be disappointed because I wasn't the kind of daughter she had in mind.

CHAPTER SEVEN

Feelings

1993

It was nearing the end of summer and the beginning of my senior year. As traditions go, summers along Lake Michigan were spent at the beach where adolescent love was discovered. Teenagers from all over came to the beach to meet new people, but avoiding the crowds was how I spent my days.

I got together with classmates sometimes, but it was annoying when they discussed boys and how they looked in their swimming trunks. There was no way I would ever share their enthusiasm regarding boys or even dating. I avoided both. The way the girls thought was not the same as me. I didn't like boys like that, and it left me feeling conflicted. Girls were supposed to like boys, get married, and have their children. That was God's intent and what I learned in church.

Aunt Sally and her friends would often meet and discuss what other people in town were doing and how it went against what God intended. When I first heard the way they talked, I was surprised and didn't realize that what they were doing was not God's intent, either.

I wasn't close to Aunt Sally, and it became an awkward situation for us. She was raising two boys and had always wanted a girl, but I didn't follow the path of a typical girl. Dresses and girlie clothes weren't my style. I found comfort in jeans, T-shirts, and hoodies. A ponytail and ball cap were what I preferred. Bows and ribbons weren't ever going to happen. It wasn't what my aunt had hoped for.

I noticed Aunt Sally's disappointment, but she never brought it up. She provided me with a safe place to stay, cared for my needs, and ensured I went to school. We didn't talk about stuff because she wouldn't understand how I felt. I had overheard Aunt Sally talking to her church friends about homosexuality and how it was a horrible sin that would get you on a direct trip to hell when you died.

Aunt Sally proudly hosted the weekly gathering of gossipers, and the attendees were women from her church. I had the unfortunate experience of overhearing Sally and her friends during one of their gatherings. On that day, the gossip was about some people who had recently moved to town.

"Did you hear about that family that just moved into the Brown's old house?" Aunt Sally asked.

"Yeah, I heard the husband is some big-city lawyer from Chicago. They say he opened his firm in Milwaukee," Penny said.

"Someone said his wife is a teacher at the elementary school," Aunt Sally added.

"Well, I heard they have a daughter who is queer, and they moved here to get her away from Chicago. They say the city is full of those people now," Lana said.

"Well, I don't want those kinds of people moving into our town," Betty Sue added.

"Did you see on the news a few months ago where them people had a Dyke March in Washington, DC, and there was one in Boston, too?" Penny said.

"What is a Dyke March?" Lana asked.

"They gather to march around different cities, rallying for equal rights so they can live in sin. If you ask me, they just want to commit their sins in the open. No one wants to see that," Penny said.

I heard them make some ridiculous noises as they all wallowed in their disgust for those people. I could imagine the foul looks and scrunched-up faces.

"Did you see that fool president on TV talking about how he will pass that Don't Ask, Don't Tell policy?" Betty Sue said.

"What's that?" Lana asked.

"Where those queers can join the military and don't have to tell people they are queer, and they can't be asked either," Betty Sue replied.

"Oh, that is awful. What about the actual soldiers? How is it fair for them to bunk in the same quarters as them queers?" Penny said.

"Well, they will have to deal with our Father in Heaven before spending an eternity in hell. No laws of man will change that," Lana said.

"They are all the devil's spawn," Aunt Sally said.

I shook my head and walked out of the kitchen. They were gross, self-righteous women. The older I got, the more I saw who they truly were and how they were wrong and not very Christian-like. They hid behind a wall of Christianity, just a façade to keep people from knowing their truth.

Penny's husband was cheating on her with Lana's sister while she fed her gambling addiction at the casino. Then there was Lana, who was cheating on her husband. I had seen him cozying up with Penny at the casino. The bank discovered that Betty Sue's daughter had been stealing money while working as a teller. Turned out her daughter had a pill addiction. And Aunt Sally? She had some skeletons in her closet that would probably be bad enough to get her kicked out of her group of devoted sinners.

They were some of the nastiest women I had ever known. I heard hours of gossiping while I was at my aunt's. When I was a kid at the farm, I would daydream of living with my aunt. I thought it would be so nice and family-like, but it turned out that life there wasn't great. Her husband was rarely around. He couldn't deal with her constant gossiping and judging of everyone in town. The things she said about other people really bothered me. Mother always said that Aunt Sally thought she was better than everyone else, and she was right.

Mother never stepped foot in a church as an adult, but she liked to fill my head with the idea that I was such a bad kid that even God didn't like me. When I heard Aunt Sally and her friends talk about homosexuality, my mind returned to my mother's words. I was so confused about my feelings, and there was no one to talk to about it.

†

I spent as much time away from my aunt's house as possible. It was an environment that I found to be uncomfortable. After Grandma was gone, it was apparent that she was the only reason the family ever came together. I felt the tension between Grandpa and Aunt Sally when he was around. She didn't really speak to him. None of it made sense to me. Grandpa was a kind man who did about anything to help others.

We remained close and spent as much time together as possible. He bought me a horse that I kept on his farm, paid for my riding lessons, and took me to all my equestrian competitions. We sometimes hung out in the shop while he worked on his cars. We talked about anything but the past.

He remarried a sweet lady named Rose. She was an amazing woman who raised her children as a single mother and took in a nephew his father had abandoned because he was too feminine. She was the most understanding woman I had ever met, and she was a true Christian who believed that God loved everyone. If only there had been more people like Rose back then. Sadly, most were like my aunt and her awful friends. They were adamant that being gay was a sin and you would spend eternity in hell. You would never convince them of anything else. It was hard to find anyone to talk to when so many people were homophobic. It was lonely. I often thought of the family my aunt and her friends were gossiping about. I wondered if the girl they talked about felt lonely too.

†

Being near the water was so calming. The beach was one of my favorite places to be, and I'd go at least a couple times a week. There was nothing like walking across the beach barefoot, something about how the sand felt between my toes. I walked down the beach to get to my favorite spot—the wind was strong.

A group of girls from my equestrian team were playing volleyball on the beach.

"Hey, Sammie, come play," I heard one of them yell.

"No thanks! I'm gonna pass." We all laughed.

The last time I played, I couldn't serve for anything. They expected me to hit the ball to the other side after they served. But that wasn't happening either. Let us just say that volleyball was not my sport. I ended up eating more sand than anything. It was rather humiliating, and I vowed never to play again.

I continued to walk. When I was almost at my favorite spot, the wind caught my cap, and it went flying down the beach. I was about to take off running after it when I saw a dark-haired girl come out of nowhere and grab it. She came toward me, and I walked toward her. We got about five feet apart when our eyes locked, and I felt a flutter in my stomach. It was a weird feeling. One I hadn't felt before.

I stood there paralyzed, unaware if I was still breathing, and she didn't look away.

What was happening? I felt different things, like her eyes were talking to me, and then a rush of panic because I wasn't sure how to react.

Finally, I looked away, breaking eye contact. I felt myself exhale, then I pointed to my cap and said, "Thank you for saving that."

"No problem," she said as she handed it to me.

After an awkward moment of silence, she said, "My name is Sarah, by the way."

I looked at her, and she was smiling. The way she studied me made me feel that flutter again, and it scared me at the same time.

I wondered if it was okay to feel those things? According to my aunt and her friends, it was wrong. But it didn't feel wrong. Why would I have those feelings if they were so wrong? It wasn't like I went looking for them. I was freaking out inside but remembered she was standing there, right in front of me...waiting for me to introduce myself.

"Oh, umm, my name is Sammie." I avoided eye contact.

"Nice to meet you, Sammie."

"Ah yes, it is nice to meet you...too." I could barely get my words out.

"Are you here alone?" she asked.

"Yeah, I mean, I know people." I pointed toward the volleyball area. "My teammates are over there playing volleyball, but it isn't my sport." I giggled like a weirdo.

"Teammates?" she asked.

"Oh yeah, from the equestrian team," I said.

"Equestrian?" she asked.

"Umm, I ride horses and compete on a team. Have you heard of dressage?" I asked.

"Like in the Olympics?"

"Yes, exactly like that." I paused. "I go to dressage competitions with my teammates."

"That is so cool," she said.

"Oh, thank you."

Fuck, I hope she doesn't think I'm an idiot.

Sarah stepped closer to me and asked, "You want to hang out?"

Oh my gosh, she wants to hang out with me. Is this real?

My mind was racing as fast as my heart, and words were not coming easily. I was so afraid of making a fool of myself, but something wouldn't let me say no.

"Ahh, sure, that would be great."

"Okay, well, so where were you headed?" she asked.

I pointed ahead of us. "There's a spot up there that is less crowded."

"Sounds perfect," she said.

We walked down the beach. I was experiencing all kinds of things inside.

"Wow, this is a great spot. Thank you for sharing it with me," she said.

"You're welcome."

My mind was in crisis mode while I processed what was going on with my body and emotions. Looking into her eyes was intense. It made me feel fluttery and my knees weak. I struggled with the thought that it was wrong to feel this way. Then I asked myself if she even felt the same or was I just freaking out for nothing?

I took a blanket and laid it out on the sand for us to sit on.

"Thank you," she said. She sat on the blanket.

"You're welcome." I sat next to her. "Have you ever been here before?"

"I came with my family when we first moved here." She looked at me. "But I like it better with you."

Every time we glanced at each other, it was intense until I looked away. I didn't know how to react and was getting frustrated with myself. I focused on listening as Sarah talked about moving here. She told me they forced her to move because her parents wanted her out of the city. I realized Sarah was the girl my aunt and her friends were talking about.

"You moved here from Chicago?"

"Yeah, how did you know?"

"My aunt and her friends are the town gossipers, and I heard them talking about a family that moved here from Chicago."

"Yeah, my parents didn't like the people I was hanging out with, and they thought *those people* changed me."

"Those people?"

"You know those queer folks. It's their fault that I have always liked girls. Funny, since I had liked girls long before I met any of my friends from the city. They made me feel comfortable because they got me."

I looked at her.

"I'm hoping you'll feel comfortable in my presence, Sammie."

Her words took my breath away and my ability to respond or speak. It was as if I didn't know how to process what she was saying and needed to let it run through my mind a time or two. Throughout that process, I sat there staring off, probably looking like a dork. I remember there were a thousand thoughts running through my mind. I wondered if she knew...

After an agonizing moment of silence, I asked, "Did you know I liked girls?"

"I didn't, but I was hoping," she said.

"Oh, I see."

That was all I could get out—*what a dumbass*. I should've said something better than *Oh, I see*.

But what should I have said? Fuck, I didn't know what to say. I was sure that was obvious.

Sarah nudged me. "Hey! Are you always this shy, or do I make you nervous?"

"Ahhh... I don't know, and I'm just not... umm, well, I don't know," I said.

Idiot, use your words!

"Relax, Sammie, just be yourself. We're just getting to know each other."

"Okay, yeah. I don't know why I'm like this."

"Like what? People get nervous, and it's human nature," Sarah said. "I would like to hang out again. You seem cool."

I was sure my face was red, but I mustered up enough nerve to say, "I think you're cool, too."

I was trying to let my walls come down a little. My nerves were becoming less intense.

There was a lot of silence between the questions we asked each other. We were both in the zone. I wondered what Sarah was thinking. Had she ever been with another girl?

"So, your parents know you're gay?"

"Yeah, but they don't support it. Not in any way. That's why they took me away from my friends in Chicago. They think I'll magically like boys now that I'm away from those evil people in the city." She shook her head. "They're so stupid. How about you? Do your parents know? Or anyone else?"

"I haven't told anyone. My parents aren't in my life. My aunt took me in years ago, and I don't think she would understand." I paused. "I heard her and her church friends talking about how queers go to hell."

"Sounds like my mother and her friends. She told me I was an embarrassment to the whole family." She rolled her eyes. "But she can't act like she has the perfect family now because I fucked that all up by being gay."

"Do you second guess your feelings?" I asked.

"No. I know what I feel and don't think anything is wrong with it." She looked at me. "How about you?"

"I've always known I liked girls, but I struggled with whether it is right."

"Right? It will never be right by those old bags from the church. They are such hypocrites. I've listened to them preach, but they aren't living by it. There is so much sinning going on in their homes."

"I never allowed myself to feel anything for anyone. I didn't think about it and mostly avoided it."

"You didn't think about it? But will you now?" Sarah asked.

I turned to look at her. "I think I will."

"Good to hear." She smiled at me, and I felt a tingle run through my body.

The time went by so fast. The sun was preparing to set. I didn't want this to end, which was a good feeling. I wondered where it would go. I didn't know, but I wanted to try because it felt so right. We both sat there quietly.

"I'm going to get to see you again, right?" she asked.

"Yes, of course." I smiled at her.

"I'm glad."

"Do you need a ride home?" I asked.

"Maybe, but can we stay for a while longer?"

"Yes, I would like that."

She said, "Thank you."

I nodded my head and looked across the lake. It was always so peaceful here. The sound of the water was relaxing. The sun set behind us as the full moon presented itself, illuminating the water while the waves rolled onto shore. Coconut... the scent of summer was in the air.

A beautiful girl sat beside me and had me feeling things I'd never felt.

It was becoming a bit chilly, but I had more blankets in my bag.

"Are you cold?" I asked.

"A little," she said.

I pulled a blanket out of the bag and handed it to her. "Here you go."

"I can't take your blanket. What are you going to use?" Sarah asked.

"I have a sweatshirt." I pulled it out of the bag.

"Maybe we should share the blanket," she said.

"Okay."

I needed to stop overthinking because it was distracting me. It was a chance meeting, and I didn't even know her. There was a connection; I felt it. My mind was filled with unwanted thoughts. I didn't want to think that way, but somehow, I always did, and it was not a fun ride.

She put the blanket over both of us and moved closer to me. My body immediately stiffened, and she felt it.

"Hey, you can relax."

When I turned to look, our eyes met, and I saw the unspoken words that brought the intensity. Sarah opened her arms wide and motioned for me to come closer as she said, "Please come here."

I got closer to her, and she pulled me in and wrapped her arms around me as she whispered, "I got you."

Human touch. It's hard to feel safe with someone in that way when you've closed yourself off to it. I didn't think about it for many years because it wasn't something I was comfortable doing. My grandparents were the only people I had ever embraced. Holding hands wasn't something I ever did.

But wow, when it didn't bring pain, it felt comforting. This felt so different, and I liked it. My body melted into her embrace. I closed my eyes, and her heartbeat was in my ear as she held me close.

"Do you feel safe now?" she whispered.

I nodded my head. It felt so safe to be wrapped up in her arms.

"It feels good to me, too, Sammie. I don't want to let go."

"Me either," I said.

We held each other for a while, savoring the feeling of being close. It was intoxicating—her scent, her touch, and how it felt to be so near to her. It was a feeling I would never forget.

Sarah was the first girl I ever loved.

It was a feeling...that couldn't be wrong.

CHAPTER EIGHT

Summer of 94

Senior Year.

It was the year that led to our freedom and adulthood. The classes seemed easy, and graduation came and went. It all flew by so fast. There were senior pictures and awkward clothing choices. Prom was another situation that became rather uncomfortable with Aunt Sally's ideas of what it should be. I skipped it and met Sarah at one of our favorite spots.

As much as we didn't want to think about it, we spent our summer that year very conscious of the fact that our time together was ending. Her family forced Sarah to go to

Connecticut that fall. It was where her mother grew up and her grandmother still lived. Her grandmother's memory was quickly slipping away. Her mother had been going back and forth because her grandmother had fallen and broken her hip. Sarah's parents decided they were going to move so her mother could be there.

"Can you go to a college here?" I knew the answer but hoped we could still see each other.

"I wish. They're making me go to the same Christian university my mother graduated from." She rolled her eyes. "I think my parents are hoping they will pray the gay out of me while I'm there."

We talked a lot about what being gay meant for us. Society was becoming more accepting of homosexuality, but my aunt and her rural American friends were not. It seemed unfair Sarah and I couldn't be our true selves without being condemned by the same people that lived a life of sin.

"They stand behind their Christianity to defend their phobias and the things they don't like or understand," Sarah said.

"Exactly! They run around cheating on their spouses and sneaking out of town to go to the casinos." I shook my head. "I can't stand them."

"Me either. We shouldn't let them win. My parents might have control now, but soon I'll move as far away from them as possible."

"Come back to Wisconsin?" I asked.

"Of course."

Sarah was fearless in so many ways. She never cared what others thought about her being gay. I wasn't as fearless. I didn't want to give anyone a reason to dislike me. Although my parents weren't in my life and had no control, my mind kept me in hiding. Aunt Sally was a helicopter parent that suffocated me, but she had no clue of who I was. I never shared my feelings with anyone back then, except for my cousin, Brandon. But he didn't know about Sarah. No one did. Until the incident.

†

Sarah and I planned a camping trip for the last weekend we had together. We spent every bit of time we could hanging out that summer. There was an overwhelming sadness that came over me every time I thought of not seeing Sarah once summer had ended. I tried to never let it show because I wanted our time together to be happy and memorable.

Our feelings were far more profound than friendship. We held hands when we were alone and would sneak off to make out. Kissing Sarah was amazing and gave me butterflies. It was the best feeling. I was excited about our trip.

I remember trying to get my jeep packed for the weekend, and Aunt Sally came outside to lecture me about being safe.

"I don't understand why you need to go alone, Sammie." She followed me around the jeep. "Who goes camping alone anyway?"

"I do. I like it that way and will be good."

I stopped, and she was right behind me.

"Are you sure you don't want Brandon to go with you?" she asked.

"Yes, I'm sure, Aunt Sally, I'll be fine."

"Well, I think it's ridiculous, Sammie."

"That's okay, you don't have to understand."

I recall wanting to get the fuck out of there because Aunt Sally was intrusive. She made me crazy with her helicopter ways. I tossed the last couple of things into the jeep and was trying to get away from her hovering.

"Take this." She handed me something. It was pepper spray. I took it and put it in the console of my jeep.

"See you soon," I said. I closed my door and hit the gas, escaping further questions.

Aunt Sally had this twisted idea of what was appropriate for girls to do. Perhaps it was because she was a boy's mom, or it was the fact that she was financially and emotionally dependent on her husband. My mother used to say she was a pampered brat who didn't know how to tie her own shoes. Whatever it was, she never got me and evidently never really grasped what life on the farm was like. If she did, she would have known that I could hold my own. At that point in my life, I never thought anything could be worse than the things that happened on the farm. But I was wrong.

†

Sarah and I met at the campsite to avoid being seen together in town. We set up camp at the site. It was our little place for those couple of days. Sara set up the stuff in the tent, and I went to get wood for our fire. I started the fire and helped Sarah get the food ready. I handed her a long fork with a hotdog on it. She just looked at me.

"Hold it over the fire, but not too close." She made me smile with her facial expressions.   We laughed when we burned our hotdogs and our marshmallows fell in the fire. Hours passed while we held hands and listened to various genres of music. We talked about the way the lyrics touched us sometimes and how music was everything. Sarah told me how she hoped to one day be a songwriter.

We had a corner site, and luckily the surrounding sites were empty, so we had the space to ourselves. In the background, we heard the hoot of the owls and the howls of the coyotes. The smell of citronella oil and campfire was in the air. Lightning bugs danced around us while the cicada's high-pitched buzz drowned out the hoots and the howls as the night passed by.

I watched her as the fire crackled and illuminated our campsite. She was so beautiful, and her dimples were so cute. I thought of how we spent the last year sneaking off to meet each other where no one would see us. We spent hours talking and holding each other as we watched the stars from the back of the jeep.

I stood and took her hand in mine.

"You wanna go walk on the beach?"

"I would love to," she said.

We walked to the beach hand in hand without a care in the world. It was a beautiful evening. The moonlight lit the shoreline as the waves crashed onto the sand. In the distance, a lighthouse with its powerful light rotated into the night, guided the ships to their ports. It was the perfect place to be.

"Hey, you want to skinny dip?" Sarah asked. "It's just you and I out here. Come on."

I looked around, and she was right. We were the only people there. She stripped her clothes off and started running toward the water.

I was more hesitant about the naked thing, so I left my bra and panties on and found the water way too damn cold. Sarah laughed at me when I squealed.

She came over, put her arms around me, and started kissing me. Suddenly, it didn't matter that the water was so frigid. I was caught up in the moment, and it felt so good until we saw headlights. Reality hit when we realized it was most likely the park ranger. We made a mad dash for our clothes as soon as the lights disappeared.

We didn't bother trying to put them on our wet bodies. Covering ourselves as much as we could, we ran toward the campsite, laughing all the way. I ran straight for the tent and grabbed a towel and tossed one to Sarah right behind me. We dried off and got dressed as fast as possible.

I sat on the edge of the air mattress and put my shoes on. "That water was freezing."

"Yes, it was. So cold," she said.

"Do you want me to get the fire going again?" I asked.

"Nah, I'm exhausted and ready to lie down."

"Okay, I'm tired too."

I kicked my shoes off and sat on the edge for a minute. My body shivered, and it must've been noticeable.

"Hey, come here and get under the blankets."

I crawled under the blankets and instantly felt the warmth of her body.

"I'll warm you up," she whispered.

She moved close to me and laid her head on my shoulder and her arm across my chest. I put my arm around her and pulled her hair from her face.

"I'm glad we're here together," she said.

"Yes, me too."

I was running my fingers up and down her arm. Her body was melting into me, and then I heard the softest snoring sounds. I remember all I could do was smile as I drifted off to sleep.

†

When I reminisced about that weekend, I thought of how I woke to the smell of the campfire lingering in the air, the sounds of the woods that surrounded us. Then I opened my eyes and looked around; Sarah was not in the tent. So I stretched and then bounced off the air mattress. I wondered what time it was and where she might've gone. I slipped on a pair of flip-flops, unzipped the tent door, and walked out.

It surprised me to see a small fire in the pit. In her hammock, I spotted Sarah with her book when I looked around. She looked at me and said, "Good Morning."

"Hey, you. You make this fire?" I asked.

"Yes, I did," she said with a smile.

"Look at you, city girl!" We both laughed.

I walked over to a chair and sat down. "So, did you sleep okay last night?"

"Yes, I slept great. Got up about thirty minutes ago. There is some cereal if you're hungry."

"I'm good for now. Do you want to do some kayaking today?"

"Yes, that sounds like so much fun."

†

We spent the day kayaking in the river, and I remember having such a great time. There was a small beach we found and stopped to have lunch. There was so much laughter. Sarah nearly lost it when I flipped my kayak. I'd never seen her laugh so hard until ten minutes later when she flipped hers. I remember not wanting it to end. It'd be our last night, and all I wanted was to make it memorable by letting down the walls completely and allowing the feelings to lead us.

When we returned to the campground, we noticed most of the sites had filled up. The groups we saw as we drove through were large, loud, and there to spend the last weekend of the summer partying. Our campsite was more secluded and off the beaten path. The surrounding people were quiet. We heard their music from time to time, and the smell of their marijuana would occasionally drift our way.

I built a fire, cooked food, and then relaxed for a few minutes. We decided we would go to the bathhouse before it was too late. We grabbed our stuff, and I asked Sarah, "You want to walk or drive up there?"

"It isn't far, right?"

"Nah, not too far."

"I'm down with walking," Sarah said.

"All right, sounds good." I grabbed a flashlight, and we headed for the bathhouse.

We met two ladies from the campsite next to ours at the bathhouse. The blonde wore a floral sundress, and the brunette wore short denim shorts and a tie-dye tank top with a giant peace sign on it. They were there with a group of friends and told us how they traveled from campground to campground throughout the United States—a group of musicians who had this extraordinary life of traveling and playing music. They asked us if we wanted to ride back with them, but we told them we would walk.

"It's about to get dark, girls," the blonde said.

"We have a flashlight," I said.

"Okay, well, be safe."

It was about ten minutes later when we came out of the bathhouse. It wasn't completely dark yet, but it was well on its way to pitch black. I grabbed the flashlight out of my bag, and we started walking back.

Someone whispered, "There they are."

"Did you hear that?" I asked.

"Hear what?"

"Maybe I'm hearing things." I looked around and didn't see anyone. "Let's just get back to camp."

The glow of campfires surrounded us while we walked through the campground. The bathhouse was in the upper section. Other camps were closer to our site but were always full and trashed by the partiers. We started down the hill that led to our campsite. The night seemed to darken as we walked through the woods.

I remember not being able to shake the feeling that someone was following us, but I refused to give in to the fear that was trying to creep in. We were a short distance from our tent, so I tried to focus on getting us there. I felt my heart beating faster and anxiety building as we walked.

When we got closer to our camp, I heard someone laugh. I felt my body stiffen when I turned around and flashed my light their way. It was three boys, and I recognized one of them. He was the brother of one girl on my equestrian team.

His name was Brad, and he was known to have anger issues after taking a bat to his girlfriend's car when she tried to break up with him. He was always getting into fights and even punched a teacher once. But his grandfather was a retired judge, and his father an assistant district attorney in a neighboring county, so he always got away with whatever he did.

The realization of the situation became clear as they continued to approach us.

"Hey queer girl, I want to talk to you," Brad said.

All three of them were making derogatory comments and stupid noises. We started walking faster. It was hard to judge how far we had to go because it was so dark, not to mention how the panic took over. We were back in the camping area as we came around the bend in the path. Our tent was nearby. The pathway was lit once we got around the corner.

I handed Sarah the flashlight and said, "I want you to get to your car and leave."

"No, Sammie, I'm not leaving you here alone."

"Look, I'm going to distract them while you get to your car, and I need you to go to the camp office and see if there is a park ranger there and bring them back. Please just get help, you understand?"

"Yes."

"Okay, you keep walking while I stop to talk to them. Get help, now, Sarah."

I turned around. "What do you need to talk to me about?"

"Where is your girlfriend going?"

"Why does it matter? You said you needed to talk to me about something," I said.

As they got closer, I could smell the alcohol in the air. I kept walking backward slowly.

"Yeah, I need to talk to you about why you're hitting on my sister."

"What?" I looked at him. I could tell he was high, and his eyes had an eerie darkness.

"I have never disrespected your sister in any way."

"Oh yeah, that's not what she told me, bitch. She told me you made her uncomfortable in the bathroom last week."

"That is not true. I never have..."

"Are you calling my sister a liar, bitch?" He charged at me.

I turned around and kept walking toward my campsite. I should've grabbed that damn pepper spray that Aunt Sally gave me. The people at the site to the north of us were not back yet. The site to the west of us was where the ladies we met at the bathhouse were. I thought if I got close enough, I could yelled for help.

As I contemplated my next move, I heard them walking behind me, talking between themselves.

"I can't believe she called your sister a liar," one boy said.

"I think this queer girl needs to be taught a lesson," Brad said.

"Yeah, I think you're right."

I recall the way my heart was beating out of my chest, but I tried to focus on getting away. I realized how alone I was. Aside from our hippy neighbors, the other campers were all Brad and Abby's friends. No one was gonna challenge Brad because of who his family was to the community.

"Hey, bitch, no one to save you now. Time for your lesson."

I ran, but someone grabbed me by the hair and pulled me to the ground. Brad ran over and sat on top of me. I struggled with him, trying to get him off me. I punched him as hard as I could in the chest. He laughed at me. Someone grabbed my arms and held them down above me. I fought as hard as I could to get out from under him, but I didn't have a chance against the three of them.

"Grab her fucking legs now," he yelled at his friend.

Brad slapped me hard across my face again and again. I still remember the burning sensation on my face and how intense it was. I could feel the gravel digging into my back under the weight of Brad. The rage inside him was coming out.

"Please stop," I screamed.

"No, fuck you. You're getting what's coming to you." He punched me in the face hard, twice. I felt the bones crack under his fist. "That's for my sister, bitch."

He ripped my shirt open and stood up. "Get her pants off," he said to his friend.

My eyes were swollen shut. I could barely see, but I could feel them ripping my clothes off. I kept begging him not to hurt me. His friends were holding my arms and legs down. I couldn't move, and he shoved something in my mouth.

The next few minutes were blurry when I thought about it. It felt like it went on forever. I had this vision of Brad on top of me, brutally assaulting my body. The pain was unbearable, but there was nothing I could've done to make it stop. It only became worse with every violent thrust from his body. I felt his hatred for me while he repeatedly had his way with me. Three big boys were holding me down. I couldn't move. All I could do was pray it would be over soon.

"I think that's enough, Brad. She can't take much more," the boy said.

"Shut the fuck up. I will say when it's enough."

I felt myself slipping away while he continued to assault my body. It had become too much.

I was fading...

I thought of the moment it stopped.

"Get the fuck off of her, now."

"Fuck you. What are you gonna do, bitches?"

"Oh fuck, they have guns."

I remember thinking I couldn't feel anything and wondering if it stopped and if they were gone. Everything was so blurry.

"Hey, you hang on, girl...we got you."

Who?

In the distance, there were voices.

"Did someone call an ambulance?"

"Yeah, the park ranger did."

Darkness...

CHAPTER NINE

A Hard Goodbye

I remember feeling so cold. Everything was blurry. It seemed so bright wherever I was and there was something on my face. I couldn't move, and there was a steady beeping sound. People were talking in the background.

"She's lost a lot of blood and has been in and out of consciousness. Her pulse is weak, her blood pressure is seventy over forty-four, and her breathing is shallow," a voice near me said.

I wondered if they were talking about me. A wave of panic came over me because I didn't know where I was or who the people talking in the background were.

Mia Barnes

I recall a ringing in my ears, and the pain was intense. There was a man talking to me and telling me everything was gonna be okay. I thought he said I was going to go to sleep for a while, but I didn't know what he meant.

I drifted off....

†

It took a few blinks for my eyes to focus. I looked around and realized that I was in a hospital room. An IV needle was in my right arm, and I had an ugly gown on. Aunt Sally was on the couch across the room with her head back and mouth wide open as she snored lightly. My cousin Brandon was relaxing in the chair next to my bed. I tried to scooch back on the bed to sit up more, but the pain stopped me, and I moaned.

Brandon jumped up. "Hey, you need to sit still, Sammie. Let me get the nurse."

He walked back into the room with a short, rather broad woman in blue scrubs. She came over to the bed and checked the monitors next to me.

"How are you feeling?" she asked.

"I've felt better."

"I bet you have, honey." She walked over and checked my IV. "What is your pain level on a scale of one to ten?"

"I don't know, a seven or eight, I guess." I shrugged my shoulders.

"All right, I'll get you something for the pain while I grab a fresh bag of fluids and antibiotics," she said.

How could I put a number on my pain? I remember thinking, *it either hurts, or it doesn't.* It hurt a lot, honestly. I

104

was afraid to move because when I did, the pain was almost too much to bear.

The nurse walked out of the room, and Brandon asked, "You okay?"

"I guess," I said.

I had hoped all this was a nightmare. The sensation of being in and out for days was overwhelming. Vague memories of Brad and his friends attacking me, but I didn't know when it ended and how I got to the hospital. I wondered if Sarah was okay, but I didn't dare ask Brandon with Aunt Sally in the room. There was no doubt the assault was real and not just another nightmare. The pain was intense, and every inch of my body hurt.

The nurse came in and attached the new bag of fluids with antibiotics and something for the pain. Before she left, she said, "What is best for you right now is rest to allow your body to heal."

She looked at Brandon and said, "No stress. The doctor will be in to check on her tomorrow."

Brandon nodded.

I closed my eyes as the medicine began to kick in. Brandon was holding my hand, and I heard him whisper, "I'm so sorry this happened to you."

The next time I woke up, I saw a doctor in the room talking to my aunt and cousin. I went to stretch out my legs, and my body yelled. The pain was still intense. The doctor walked over to my bed when he heard me moving around.

"Hello, Ms. Wilson, I'm Doctor Scott," he said as he reached out and shook my hand. He was a tall man with salt-and-pepper hair and blue eyes. The way my aunt looked at him made me uncomfortable for him.

"Hello," I responded.

"How are you feeling this morning?"

"Okay."

"Okay, doesn't help me determine how I can help your pain, Ms. Wilson. Can you give me a number between one and ten?"

The number game again. How about it hurts like hell, and I don't want to be here? I don't want to give you a fucking number between one and ten. IT HURTS.

That is what I wanted to say, but I responded with, "I guess I would say a nine."

He nodded. "We can get you something more for the pain."

He asked if I wanted my aunt in the room while he talked to me about my injuries, and I told him no. Brandon led his mother out of the room.

The doctor explained my facial injuries included an orbital fracture, which would heal on its own. The pain in my jaw was caused by a zygomatic break.

"I consulted with a maxillofacial surgeon who recommended surgical reduction with fixation. He'll be by later to explain the procedure."

I had extensive vaginal bruising with tearing that required a procedure to repair lacerations. There were five staples in the back of my head from an injury I didn't remember. My body was peppered in bruises from the attack.

The doctor told me that they wanted to do the procedure on my cheekbone the following day. He said that if all went well, I'd be able to leave in a couple days.

The doctor reached out and touched my hand. "Young lady, I'm truly sorry you have to go through all of this. Your injuries are going to take some time to heal." He paused for a moment. "Do you have a therapist you talk to?"

"No."

"I'll have the patient advocate bring you some information. I recommend talking to someone."

I nodded my head. That was not high on my list. Talking to a stranger was not something I was comfortable with.

The doctor walked out of the room.

I lay there trying to remember. Everything was so blurry. *Did Sarah make it back? I hope she is okay.* I wished I could remember more, but I just kept drawing blanks.

Why did this happen?

Brandon walked into the room. "Hey, Sam! How are you feeling?" he asked.

"My body hurts, my head throbs, and I'm here where I don't want to be."

Aunt Sally was behind Brandon, and she walked up to my bed. She had no makeup on, which wasn't normal for her. Her hair was a mess, not done up as usual. She was wearing a running suit, and her eyes looked puffy. Aunt Sally looked pissed, to be honest. She stood there looking at me and asked, "Sam, what were you thinking?"

"What do you mean? What was I thinking?" I asked. Before she could answer, I said, "I did nothing to deserve what they did. I did nothing wrong."

She stood there staring at me. "You know what I mean, and you were with that queer girl."

"Yeah, I was. We're friends."

"Dishonorable passions." The look on her face was disturbing.

"Whatever." I wasn't going to go into it with her because there was a long list of dishonorable acts my aunt and her friends committed.

"Mother, that's enough," Brandon said.

"And since they did not see fit to acknowledge God, God gave them up to a debased mind to do what ought not be done," she hissed as she recited Romans 1:28.

"Mother, I said that's enough."

Aunt Sally shook her head. "I'm going to leave now. Brandon, I need you to take care of what we discussed, and it needs to happen soon." She looked at me again. Her eyes were cold and resembled my mother's. It gave me chills. I looked away, and she turned around and walked out of the room. It was obvious from the way she looked at me that I disgusted her. What happened to me embarrassed her. I was sure it caused a ripple effect amongst her social circles and church.

†

I returned to Aunt Sally's after five days in the hospital. It was an awkward situation, and I spent most of my time in my room because it was difficult to be there. I tried to reach Sarah, but her phone went straight to voicemail.

Grandpa and Rose came to visit. Rose was so sweet. She told me not to let what happened change who I was. I don't think she understood how people stared at me now— including my family.

When we went to my doctor's appointment, Aunt Sally deliberately went a long way around to avoid her friends seeing her with me in the car. She didn't say that, but I knew that was what she was doing. My aunt barely acknowledged me and would not look at me even when she spoke to me. I was pretty sure she hated me.

Grandpa took my hand, and I looked at him. "I'm sorry this happened to you, Sammie."

I squeezed his hand and said, "I know you are, but it isn't your fault."

We visited for a while, and then Grandpa said, "You girls visit without me. I'm going to go talk to Sally."

Rose looked at me and smiled.

"I'm pretty sure she doesn't want me here anymore. She's disgusted and she won't even look at me."

"Well, honey, we all know it is because her high and mighty friends have been in her ear," Rose said in a matter-of-fact tone.

She was right. What Aunt Sally's friends thought and said was all that mattered to her. The fact she had the devil's spawn living in her house had created much drama for her. Suddenly, there was yelling coming from the other room.

"I can't have her living in my house, Dad. She's humiliated our family," she said. Her tone got louder.

"Oh, for God's sake, Sally, she's a child who was brutally attacked by some out-of-control young man who will never be charged," he said.

"She is not a child, Dad. She is a young adult who chose to commit sinful acts," she shot back at him.

"Sally are you suggesting she deserved what happened to her?" he asked. "You didn't have a problem taking that man's blood money to keep his son out of trouble. Funny how it's only a sin if you aren't doing it."

"Dad, I don't want to talk to you about this anymore. I want her out of my house by the end of the week."

Rose just looked at me with pity in her eyes. I didn't want to be there any more than Sally wanted me there. Aunt Sally's home had always been temporary and safer than where I came from, but she never understood me, and this town was not where I needed to be.

†

I remember Grandpa coming back the following day. He walked into the room, and my cousin Brandon was right behind him. It seemed odd, but many things had been strange since the incident. Brandon shot me a goofy smile, and I felt slightly more at ease. We had always been close; he was four years older than me. A gentle soul. Even as a teenager, he never stopped looking out for me. He once asked me if I liked girls and told me if I did, it was okay. He didn't care. We didn't hang out as much as we did when I first arrived because he got a girlfriend, Cara, but I knew he was always on my side.

"What do you guys want?" I asked.

"Rose told me you heard what Sally said when I was talking to her yesterday," Grandpa said.

"Yeah, we heard what she said," I responded. "But I already knew that was coming."

"Well, Sammie, I find her way of thinking repulsive, so don't worry," Brandon said.

"Me, too," Grandpa added as he took my hand.

"Don't worry about my crazy ass mother, Sammie. She isn't right in her damn head."

"We want to pass something by you," Grandpa said. He nodded at Brandon.

"Cara and I are moving to New Mexico. I found a job down there, and we're moving this weekend. We were talking last night, and she asked if you would like to come with us. She found an amazing house with a spare room that could be yours," Brandon said.

"What do you think, Sammie?" Grandpa asked. "Rose and I will visit often, and you can start a new life for yourself."

I asked if I could talk to Brandon privately, and Grandpa excused himself from the room.

"Come on, Sammie, come with us and get a new start," Brandon said.

"Are you sure Cara is okay with this, Brandon?" I asked.

"For sure, she is the one that suggested it," he said with a smile.

"You aren't just saying that I hope. I know your mother pressured you to get me out of here. She's done the same with Grandpa, but I don't want to be a burden to anyone. I'm an adult now."

"Just hush. Cara, and I want you there because we love you like a little sister. I don't give a damn about what my mother wants, and she crossed some lines that she can't uncross with me."

"Brandon, can I ask you something?"

"Go for it."

"Can you find a way to get a hold of Sarah so I can see her before I go?"

"Well, you know I'll try, Sammie. Does this mean you are going with us?"

"Yeah, I'm going with you. Please tell Cara thank you for me," I said.

"Of course." He hugged me before leaving.

†

Brandon came through with arranging a visit with Sarah. I wasn't sure how, but I wasn't going to ask questions. I was just happy I could see her again. He organized a meeting at a restaurant in Illinois. Sarah's brother was the one that brought her. Brandon walked up and shook his hand.

Brandon said, "You two find a table so you can talk. The three of us will visit over here for a bit."

We walked over to a corner booth and sat down across the table from each other.

"Wow, your brother brought you?" I asked.

"Your cousin talked to him, and he told him he would bring me to see you before you leave." She paused. "On the way here, he told me he was sorry about what happened to you and that our parents are homophobes."

"Well, I appreciate him for bringing you. I've been so worried about you."

"Worried about me, Sammie?" She raised her eyebrows. "You're the one that got hurt, not me. I should've never left you there," she said.

"No, you had to go get help, Sarah. It could have been both of us and who knows how it would have ended," I said. She looked down, and I asked, "Were they still there when you came back?"

"It seemed like it took forever for me to get help. The park ranger wasn't there, so I called the police on the phone

112

in front of the office. The park ranger showed up before the police, so he had his wife stay behind to wait for them." She paused. I could tell she was about to cry by her face, so I reached across the table and took her hand. "When we got close to where you were, we could see Brad kicking you in the stomach and chest. But then, out of nowhere, those women we met at the bathhouse were there holding guns on them. The three of them took off with their tails between their legs. One woman covered you with a blanket," Sarah said.

"I ran over to you. Brad hurt you so bad." She put her head down.

"I'm okay, Sarah. So how did I get to the hospital, and did the police get Brad?"

"Ambulance transported you, and I was with you."

"It was you beside me. I knew someone was with me, but everything is so blurry."

"Yes. I was with you in the ambulance, and I stayed with you at the hospital as long as I could before my parents made me leave." She paused. "The police got there, but he was gone, and his friends, too."

"Of course, they were," I said. "Thank you for staying with me."

"I wanted to be there. I'm so sorry, Sammie."

"Sarah, it wasn't your fault. You did what I needed you to do."

"But Sammie, you wouldn't have been there if it wasn't for me," she cried.

"I was there because I wanted to be, Sarah. What happened is not your fault."

"Sammie, you don't understand."

"So, tell me what I don't understand," I said.

She looked at me with a look that I had not seen before. What was this thing she thought I didn't understand?

"You know why we moved here. I told you all of that."

I nodded.

"Well, my dad is good friends with Brad's father. They went to college together," she said.

"Okay. So, you know Brad?" I asked.

"Not really. I haven't seen him since we were toddlers," she said. "But I guess when we moved here from the city, Dad went to Brad's father and asked him to have his son pursue me."

"What?"

"Yeah, to convince me I wasn't gay."

"Wow, did he ever approach you?" I asked.

"No, he never had the chance. He was supposed to make his move that day I met you on the beach."

"Oh, so that's why he hates me."

"Yeah, that, and when his dad found out what happened, he told Brad he would never be a man. He told him he was an embarrassment to the family because he was weak and couldn't get me away from a queer."

"That explains his hatred for me. Wait, did you know about this before...."

"No. I found out from my brother, who had heard our father talking about it. He said Brad started drinking a lot after his father outed him at a family gathering. His mother told the ladies at church that she was afraid he would blow one day and hurt someone."

"That makes more sense to me and explains why he wanted to hurt me," I said to Sarah.

She nodded and said, "I'm so sorry, Sammie."

"Please don't be. What Brad did was not because of anything you did. It happened because I'm queer."

"But it's who I am, too, and I approached you."

"It doesn't matter. It happened, and all we can do is heal from it."

She nodded her head and wiped a tear from her cheek. "Thank you for making my stay in that God-forsaken town more bearable, Sammie."

"The same to you, Sarah. I'll be happy to be away from there forever. I'm just sorry I won't get to see you anymore."

"I know, but you'll find some awesome girl and forget all about me."

"Don't say that. I'll never forget you, Sarah."

She was my first love. I'll never forget our time together.

She looked at me, and there was a tear running down her face. We embraced one last time, and she started walking toward her brother. She turned around briefly and paused, but no words were spoken. We just walked away from each other.

The hardest goodbye... I never said.

CHAPTER TEN

Half Alive

June 2016

There was a loud banging noise in the hallway. I opened my eyes, and my room was so bright.

Why were my blinds open?

My head was pounding, and the bright light was too much. What the hell was that noise? Through my squinting eyes, I saw Zoë walk into my line of vision.

"Good morning, gorgeous!" Zoë said.

"Fuck, Zoë, too early. Please shut my blinds."

"Nope, there are things to do. Like, hydrate yourself!"

My frontal lobe had a pain that was screaming. The ability to think didn't exist. My mouth was so dry. "What the hell happened last night?" I asked.

"Three bottles of wine."

"Fuck," I said.

I stumbled to the bathroom to brush the disgusting taste out of my mouth.

Judging by my reflection in the mirror, I looked as bad as I felt. My makeup was all over, and my eyes were all puffy. I grabbed a cloth, ran cool water on it, and wrung it out. As I laid it on my face, the fabric felt refreshing against my skin. After I washed and patted it dry, I looked in the mirror. "Better," I whispered.

I walked to the kitchen. On the bar next to the freshly cut flowers sat a cup of coffee, waiting for me.

I sat on a bar stool. I looked at Zoë. "Thank you."

"Of course. Would you like some toast to go with your ibuprofen?" She giggled.

"Ha ha, you're so funny. Yes, I would love some toast, and if you could direct me to the ibuprofen, that would be great." I put my head in my hands and whined, "I hate hangovers. Did I mention that?"

"Yeah, maybe once or twice," she said.

I looked at the flowers on the bar. "These are beautiful. Where did you get them? And do not tell me the neighbor's yard!"

She laughed and said, "I got them at that little floral place on the corner, across from the coffee shop downtown."

"You did well."

"Thank you. I thought it would be nice to brighten the place up a bit."

"Agreed!"

I got a few bites of toast down, but I was still feeling rough.

"I think I'm going to hit the couch for a bit. My head is not okay," I said to Zoë.

I couldn't believe I drank that much. Hangovers were the worst, especially those that came from too much wine. I walked over to the end of the couch and plopped down. There was a soft purple blanket laid over the couch. I grabbed it and threw it over me.

Zoë walked into the living room and over to me as I settled on the couch. She handed me a water bottle and said, "You're gonna wanna drink all of this."

"Why'd you let me drink so much last night?"

"Like I can stop you, Sam." We laughed.

"I just remember talking, and then I wake up to your shenanigans and the worst headache ever. And let's not even talk about the taste in my mouth."

Zoë laughed. "It will pass, I promise, but you have to get fluids in!"

"Ugh, I hear you." I grabbed my water and took a drink. The cold felt good on the back of my throat.

"You get some rest. I'm going to run errands, and then we can take care of business later."

I closed my eyes. Sleep was the only thing that was going to make me feel better!

†

I laid there for a moment, taking in the smells that had awoken my senses and stomach. I wanted to open my eyes, but I just laid there evaluating how I felt before I got up. My headache wasn't as loud. It seemed my hunger was back in full force, and I needed some of whatever that smell was coming from the kitchen. I wondered what time it was. I felt like I had been sleeping forever. As I wandered through the house to the kitchen, I passed a mirror in the hall. *Damn, I'm looking rough.* I wasn't sure I cared at that point.

Zoë turned around and asked, "Are you feeling better?"

I sat on the stool and responded, "I think so. What time is it?"

Zoë looked at her watch. "It's 12:37. You slept a couple of hours."

"I don't know what you are making, but it smells so good."

I didn't know how it happened, but Zoë learned how to cook some fantastic meals. When we met, she couldn't cook a box of mac and cheese. Now she made these amazingly delicious meals from recipes she one day decided to try.

"So, I just made some bacon for an avocado BLT, and I made a broccoli pasta salad earlier today. You interested?" she asked.

"Oh my God, yes! I love you, Zoë!"

"You mean you love my cooking?"

I smiled at her. "You know I love you, but your cooking is the cherry on top!"

"Shut up, dork." She handed me a plate.

†

A lot had changed since I came back almost a year ago. The rehab story brought me here, but meeting Lexi and

119

confronting my past altered the direction of my life and put me on a healthier path that allowed me to be true to myself. My relationship with Zoë was changing and becoming deeper. The walls were collapsing, but the way I processed things was not exactly healthy. It was very difficult for me to receive positive things said to me or about me. It literally weirded me out, and my vibe got awkward. I didn't know how to react to the positive. It was easier to avoid it, if possible.

If someone liked me, I feared I would do something that would make them change their mind. My mind was fucked, and when I was attracted to someone, it took me on a rollercoaster ride of doubts, overthinking everything. I couldn't find a safe place where I could land and feel like I could breathe. It was a constant rush of thoughts that all cast doubts, leaving me afraid to let anyone in.

I hated those thoughts. I did everything possible to stop them from getting at me. But fear and doubt would always win if I didn't find a different way of thinking. What I knew for sure was that I didn't want to lose Zoë.

✝

Zoë and I flew back to New Mexico in early November. The magazine issue with Lexi's story came out in October and received overwhelmingly positive feedback. My email inbox was filling up with requests for us to speak at events about domestic violence. We scheduled a few speaking events to see if it was something we wanted to continue to do. So far, it had been good, and Lexi was blossoming, and she saw how telling her story helped others.

While in New Mexico, I met with Zoë's team to brainstorm ideas for her website and blog. I had been doing content writing for her businesses for years. The best part of being a freelance writer was choosing for whom I wanted to write and what content I wanted to write.

We flew back to the Milwaukee area in late May to stay for a few months. Lexi's story won a National Magazine award, increasing the number of requests for us to speak at events. Zoë had some projects in the area, too. Life was moving on. We decided we wanted a few days off to relax and hang out at the beach when we returned to Wisconsin. We planned to drive to a lighthouse that was recently opened for tours. It was about an hour and a half north of Milwaukee, a beautiful drive up the shore. We stopped for lunch, and I consumed enough alcohol to decide to bare my soul to Zoë that night. The next day I woke up feeling like the walking dead and had my best friend wanting to converse further about what I said in my drunken stupor. I would've done anything to avoid any further conversation about my moment of weakness.

After we finished lunch, Zoë asked, "You feel better?"

"Yes, the food helped, thank you," I said.

"Of course. You want to go to the beach?"

I looked at her, and she looked at me and smiled.

"I'd love to relax on the beach for sure," I said.

†

It was another beautiful June day in Milwaukee, and the beaches were full of families. We found a spot to set up our chairs and umbrellas. I loved being on the beach. The sounds of the waves hitting the shore were so serene. There were also the sounds of seagulls squawking in the background as they fought over the remnants of food left behind by visitors. I laid back in the chair, taking in the sun, and the light breeze danced across my skin.

Zoë squealed and said, "Get away, shoo."

I opened my eyes and saw a seagull next to Zoë, looking at her chips, and I started laughing.

"He just wants a chip," I said.

"He needs to go get his own, now shoo." The seagull finally flew away, and Zoë said, "Those damn birds are always trying to get my food."

I laughed. "Yup, that's what they do. Just be glad they haven't shit on you yet."

"Yet?"

"Oh, it will happen eventually."

"They better not."

I just smiled, then laid back again and closed my eyes. I didn't feel one hundred percent yet and considered never drinking again. Being at the beach helped. It was a great place to relax.

"So, Sammie, I wanted to talk to you about some things," Zoë said.

Oh, no! Here we go. She's going to want to talk about what I said last night.

"What do you want to talk about?" I asked.

"Earlier, I called a realtor I know in this area to look at places. I was wanting to find a place to rent on the shore. She has some available with a six-month lease that she told me about. At first, I was thinking about renting, but after talking to my friend, there are some investment properties I'm going to look at next week. It would be nice to have a place to come up here whenever we want."

"Are you serious?" I looked at her.

"When we were talking last night, you said you want to stay longer. I think you should stay as long as you need. I want to be here with you." She paused for a moment. "She found a few places near the lake available to rent on a six-month contract. We can go by and look at them. I hope to have a place bought and renovated by then."

I looked at her and asked, "Six months? Zoë, don't you need to get back to New Mexico?"

"You don't want me here?"

"No, that isn't it. What about work?" I asked.

"Mom and Tom are running the real estate office, and I can do business from here. I'll likely have to travel back a few days occasionally, but otherwise, I'm able to do it all while staying here. I'm gonna stay so you have someone with you while you write your book."

"Write my book?" I looked at her.

"Have you forgotten the conversation from last night?"

The memories were blurry. I vaguely remembered our discussion about the farm, during which I cried and told Zoë I didn't want her sympathy. But there seemed to be a lot more that I didn't remember, and that was scary.

I looked over at her and said, "I suspect I did too much talking."

"Whatever, Sam. You can't say that now. I appreciate you trusting me and opening up. It helps me understand you more and the things you struggle with. With the people you've had in your life, it's no wonder you don't trust people. I would be afraid to let people in, too, after Natalie's bullshit. She was a real bitch."

Why did I bring up Natalie to Zoë?

"I don't want to be viewed as some victim, Zoë. We all have a past, and we all go through some shit. I've moved on with my life," I said.

"Moved on with your life, Sammie? You don't get to call half-alive living."

"What the fuck is that supposed to mean, Zoë? I'm out here doing things no one ever thought I could do."

"Yes, for sure you have, and I'm positive you'll keep doing great things. But that's not what I'm talking about."

"Okay. Do I want to know?"

"Well, you need to know, Sammie, because your fear of love and intimacy holds you back from a full life. When someone touches you, you stiffen, and you avoid eye contact when the conversation shifts to feelings."

I stared off at the lake. I heard her, but I didn't know what to say. She wasn't wrong, but I had no idea how to get past it.

"You deserve love and to feel it in its entirety. I always wondered why you were so shut off from it. I thought it was me, especially when you ended up with Natalie. But now I get it, and neither your family nor Natalie gave you a reason to believe you are worth it. But I'm beside you, telling you that you are worth love, happiness, and the best life you can have."

She put her arm around me, pulled me closer, and said, "Sam, it's okay to need to heal and to confront the demons that hold you back. You don't always have to be okay. It's okay to need someone to lean on, Sammie."

124

I leaned into her and rested my head on her chest. When I closed my eyes, I could hear her heart beating. I found so much comfort in being in Zoë's arms. I realized as I developed as a person, so did my feelings. The time had come for me to love fearlessly because my person was right there beside me. I could not blow this.

Zoë squeezed me. "Hey Sam, stop overthinking stuff."

I looked at her and asked, "Who said I'm thinking anything?"

"Your toes are all curled up. That's an indicator that you are overthinking."

"Whatever, you're a weirdo. And I hate not knowing everything I said to you."

"You don't need to stress yourself over that. You're safe with me."

"I just hate losing control and not remembering what I said."

"Stop worrying!" She stood up. "I'm going to go jump in the lake for a minute."

"All right, I'll be here watching to see how cold the water might be!" I said as she ran off.

Lake Michigan water never really got warm. It was tolerable to swim in when it was hot outside. Many people swam in it, but I was not one of them. I would only go so deep and turn around. I sat on the shore and let the waves wash over me, but I was not interested in being in the water much because the undertow scared me.

Zoë jumped right in and took off swimming. When she resurfaced, she gave me a thumbs up. I laughed. There was no way I was going in the water. She returned quickly and grabbed her towel. "Okay, so maybe it is a bit chilly!"

"You think?" I laughed.

"Oh my gosh, it is freezing. How do people swim in there?"

"I don't know. It is beautiful but always so cold!" Zoë wrapped herself in her towel. She was so adorable. "You ready to get out of here?" she asked.

"Yes, I'm ready."

We passed a bar and grill on the water as we drove back to the house.

"Hey, that place looks cool," Zoë said.

"Want to check it out for dinner?" I asked.

"Sounds like a plan," she responded.

✝

We walked into the bar and grill. It was a Friday night, so there were a lot of people there. I looked at Zoë, and she said, "We're going to sit down and eat. No backing out now."

"Just two?" the man at the door asked.

We both nodded, and he said, "Okay, give me a moment."

A few minutes later, he walked us to a table on the deck. It was a great night to sit out there. The moon was full and illuminating the water. I could hear the waves hitting the pier close by. Not that we could hear much over the group of women at the bar. They were all dressed like they were going to the club down the street. The ladies had on glittering dresses and tops, three-inch stilettos, long gaudy nails, and there was a lot of hair tossing. They all had one volume as they puffed on their long, skinny cigarettes. Soon they went inside to play pool, and it got quiet enough to continue our conversation about staying in the Milwaukee area.

"So, while you were in the shower, I called to make appointments for us to see the three rentals I found. I think it will be better to make an appointment than just drive by. Are you down?"

"Yes, that will work. When are the appointments?"

"I scheduled them for next Monday because you don't have anything on your calendar."

"You are something else, Zoë." I smiled.

"That's what I hear!" She laughed.

We were finishing our dinner when a large group came in and were seated at the other end of the deck. Zoë and I decided we wanted to play some pool, so we got up and walked into the other area of the bar. We avoided the enormous group and made our way to the pool tables.

Zoë quickly laid claim to one table, and the fun began. She could put on quite a performance when we went out and didn't give a shit what people thought. Zoë moved behind me and put her arms around me while showing me how to take the shot—not because she had to. She thought it was funny. When I looked up, I saw two men staring at us. I looked away and moved on to my next attempt.

We played a few more games, and I avoided looking at the staring men. When I mentioned to Zoë that they were creeping me out, she said, "They're probably just checking us out, like men do."

"Hey, I need to go to the ladies room. You want to go with?"

"No, I'm good. I'll stay with our stuff."

"Okay then, I'll be right back," she said.

I picked up my phone to look at my Instagram until I felt someone coming toward me. I looked and saw a woman with long curly auburn hair, wearing a cowboy hat, a white shirt, jeans, and white boots. She seemed familiar, and so did the lady that walked with her. She had short dark hair and was dressed like her friend.

"Hey, aren't you Samantha Wilson?" the woman with auburn hair asked.

"Yeah, that's me." I paused for a moment and then asked, "Do I know you?"

"Abby York and Candy Edwards. We were on the Equestrian team with you."

Abby avoided eye contact and looked away as Candy kept talking, but I didn't hear her because as soon as she said their names, I felt panic. Oh my God, I needed Zoë to come back soon. The tingling sensation ran up my arms as a sudden heavy feeling in my chest and a wave of nausea hit.

"Samantha, are you okay?" Candy asked.

"Ahh, yes, I'm good." I looked and saw Zoë walking up.

She approached and touched my arm. "Sam, are you good?" she asked.

"Yeah, I'm good."

Silence, awkward silence. Until one of the ladies spoke. "Hello, I'm Candy, and this is Abby. We were on the equestrian team with Samantha a long time ago."

"Okay, I see," she said awkwardly.

"This is Zoë."

"We heard you were in town," Candy said to me.

I nodded my head and said, "Yeah, here for work."

"I've read some of your work. It's impressive," Candy said.

"Thanks," I said. The interaction couldn't have been any more uncomfortable.

Abby stared off, and we avoided eye contact.

A man from across the bar yelled, "Candy, get your ass over here! It's your turn."

She looked at me and said, "It was good to see you, Sam."

"Yeah," I mumbled.

They returned to their group. Candy was whispering in Abby's ear, and she turned around and looked at me. I stood there deep in thought. Zoë whispered, "What just happened?"

I looked at her and shook my head. "Do you mind if we get out of here?"

"No, not at all."

We walked out the side door and up the boardwalk toward my car.

"Sam, what is up with those women?"

"They are just people from my past, Zoë."

"Why do you look so freaked out?"

Before I could answer, a male voice came up behind us. "Hey, where are you going, dyke?"

I briefly turned around and saw Brad, Abby's brother. His hair was thick and shaggy, just as I remembered. The same bull-legged strut in rugged jeans and cowboy boots. Slumped shoulders in a tight-fitting t-shirt over a beer gut. I saw the look on his face, and I knew what was coming next. Brad and alcohol equaled a giant, aggressive asshole.

I looked at Zoë and said, "Please just ignore him and let's get to my car."

We picked up the pace and walked toward the car. I heard Candy say, "Hey, leave them alone. Why do you always gotta fuck with someone, Brad?"

"Shut up, Candy, get back inside," Brad yelled.

"Brad, stop, leave them alone." I heard a female voice say.

"Abby, go inside," he said.

We got to the car, and I saw him walking toward us. "Zoë, stay in the car, please."

"Hey, Sammie, you and your dyke girlfriend think you're too good?" he asked.

"That's it," Zoë said.

She jumped out of the car and walked toward him. "Look motherfucker, I don't know what your problem is, but go fuck with someone else."

He shoved Zoë back. She jumped back up, and he punched her hard in the face. She fell back. I jumped out and grabbed her, and tried to get her back in the car.

"Well, I can see you didn't learn anything from last time," Brad said to me.

Zoë tried to pull away from me.

"No, Zoë." I opened the car door. "You're gonna get in the fucking car."

She sat in the seat, and I leaned in the car and grabbed my handgun out of the glove box. "Stay right here." I shut her door.

He continued to come toward me. I pointed my gun at him.

"Look, you need to back the fuck off, now." I walked around the car toward my door. The gun was pointed at him, and he stopped. I looked and saw a crowd gathering outside the pub. They were all staring as I continued to point my gun at Brad.

"Get back," I yelled.

"What the fuck?" he said.

"You just back the fuck up. Let us leave, and there will be no problems," I said.

I opened my door, slowly got in, started the car, and quickly drove away as the crowd stood in disbelief.

I looked over at Zoë when we got down the street. There was blood running down her face.

"Oh my God, Zoë. Are you okay?" I asked.

"My head hurts, but I think I'll live."

I grabbed a towel from the back seat and handed it to Zoë.

"Sam, who was that man?"

"A demon from my past," I said.

CHAPTER ELEVEN

Vulnerability

It was as if something had taken over me. Never again would that man hurt me or someone I loved. When we drove away, I looked down at the handgun still lying in my lap. Both my hands gripped the steering wheel tightly while I replayed what had just happened in my mind. Why did that man still hate me after all these years? I looked over at Zoë. She had the towel pressed against her face to stop the bleeding.

"Oh God, Zoë, I'm so sorry you got caught up in this," I said to her.

"Sam, you didn't do this. Stop apologizing for shit that isn't your fault," she said.

I reached over and took her hand. "Thank you for having my back, Zoë."

She squeezed my hand.

We pulled into the driveway, and I parked. I grabbed my gun, made sure the safety was on, and slipped it into my waistband. Then I went around to help Zoë out of the car.

We walked into the house, and I saw Zoë's face in the light. "Oh God, you might need to see a doctor." I cringed at the sight of the gash above her eye.

"No way, I'm not going near any hospital where there are sick people and their germs." She sat down at the bar. "You have a first aid kit?"

I walked over, set my gun on the counter, and said, "You are such a hardhead, Zoë."

"Paid off in this situation, didn't it?" She laughed.

I walked away, chuckling as I got the first aid kit from the bathroom. As I walked through the kitchen, I stopped by the fridge to grab a couple of beers. I handed Zoë one and said, "You might need this!"

She looked at me and said, "What exactly do you plan on doing?"

I laughed.

I cleaned the gash above Zoë's eye and put butterfly strips on it. There was so much swelling around her eye with a mixture of blue and purple bruising. "This gash is so deep, Zoë. I would feel better if you saw a doctor," I said.

"Sammie, I'm good. It's stopped bleeding. Now I just need some ibuprofen and a place to rest my head.

"And some ice for that eye." I looked at her and felt so bad Brad hit her because of me.

I prepared an ice pack for her. When I turned around to hand it to her, she asked, "Sammie, who was that man?"

"His name is Brad, and I haven't seen him since the summer that..." I paused. "Hey, you need to lay your head down."

"I will." She paused and pointed at the gun. "And when did you get that?"

"I've had it for a while." I picked it up. "Be right back, gonna put this up now."

When I walked back into the room, Zoë said, "Let's sit on the couch. I can lay my head back and ice my eye."

"Okay."

I wasn't really up for a conversation about Brad, but I knew she wouldn't let it go that easily, and she had the right to know why she ended up with a gash on her head.

We sat on the couch, and Zoë laid her head on my lap and placed the ice on her head. I made sure she was comfortable before I got into the details of Brad.

"Why don't you rest, and we can talk about stuff later."

"Nice try, Sammie. I'm resting right here on your lap. Please tell me who that dickhead man is and why he was fucking with you."

I told her about meeting Sarah, the time we spent together, and our last camping trip before she went to Connecticut.

"You never saw Sarah again?"

"Just once."

"So, she was your first?"

"The first person I had feelings for, but never..." I shook my head.

"Why?"

"My stupid fears, I had hoped that night we would act on our feelings, but..."

I explained to her the events of that night, my aunt's response, and the reason for Brad's deep-seated hatred of me.

"Why the fuck is he not in prison, Sammie?"

"Because his dad was an assistant district attorney, and he was never charged," I answered.

The look on her face said it all, and she was mad as hell.

"You're telling me he never paid for what he did?"

"He never paid. But his dad sent my aunt a nice big check to keep it quiet."

"What about you?"

"My aunt banished me. She was mad as hell at me for being queer. My cousin and his wife invited me to stay with them in New Mexico while I went to college. It all worked out."

"You think it all worked out?"

"It was a long time ago, Zoë. I don't want to hang onto it and give him that power."

Zoë sat up and looked at me. "I get that, Sammie, I do. Thank you for letting me in. I know it's hard for you to be vulnerable." She grabbed my hand. "I'm so sorry you've had to deal with so much."

"I don't want to be pitied."

"Fuck, I don't pity you, babe. I look at you and admire the woman that sits here beside me. You are a tough cookie, a survivor, but it's okay not to be all right sometimes."

"Okay, speaking of tough cookies, you need to go to bed and get some rest," I said.

"If you come with me to snuggle, I'll go to bed."

I looked at her, and she was giving me a look I couldn't say no to, so I smiled. "All right, I'll snuggle with you. Let me change, and I'll see you in a minute."

Snuggling was something Zoë and I often did. The love we had for each other came with a lot of respect, and when one of us was having a shit day, we found comfort in each other. It was a good feeling to have someone like Zoë in my corner.

†

I ran down the beach. My flip-flops flew off when I first started running. They were in front of me now, too. There was nowhere to go. The rumble of laughter was coming from the crowd. I ran in circles, trying to find my escape. I felt something hit me in the head, and I turned around. Everyone was just laughing as they surrounded me. The crowd was closing in on me. Words were the weapons of choice, taking me to my knees. "No, PLEASE, stop. Don't do this, please!" *I yelled.*

Breathe, just breathe, I tried to tell myself... It was dark. Why was it so dark....

"Sammie, hey, it's okay, you're okay," a voice said to me.

Someone touched me. I jumped and opened my eyes.

"Hey. You were yelling out. Are you okay?" she asked.

"Yeah, I'm good." Oh my God, it was just a bad dream. My head felt fuzzy. There was a wet sensation on my cheek. *No, no tears.* She couldn't see me like that. I looked away and quickly wiped the tear.

"Hey you, come here," she said.

136

"I'm okay, Zoë. It was just a dream."

"Come here, Sam." She had her arms reaching out to me. I let her take me into her arms.

"It's okay to need someone, Sammie. It doesn't mean you're weak," she said.

Sometimes it was as if she knew what I was thinking. It felt good to have someone embrace me. Sleep came fast.

†

I was digging through the cupboards when Zoë walked into the kitchen.

"What are you looking for, babe?" she asked.

"Oh, my travel mug. I was going to take coffee with me, so I don't have to stop, but I have no idea where I put it."

"Dishwasher," she said.

She moved through to the laundry room. I shook my head. I was going to need to make my coffee strong!

Zoë came back through the kitchen and sat on the stool. I turned around and saw her double shiner and her gnarly gash.

"Damn, Zoë, are you feeling okay?"

"Yeah, my head is a little tender, but I took some ibuprofen, and it's tolerable. I just can't bend over because it makes my head throb."

"You should relax on the couch and take care of yourself for a day," I said.

"So, what you got on your agenda today?" she asked.

"I'm headed to kick some demon ass and do a little research for my book."

"Oh yeah? Are you ready to do it by yourself?" she asked.

"Yes, Zoë," I snapped.

"Damn, sorry I asked," she said.

"I'm not going to break, Zoë."

"I know you're not, Sam, but I'm not the fucking enemy." She got up from the bar stool and walked to her room.

Being snappy with Zoë wasn't okay, but I never wanted to be perceived as weak or needy. I hated that she saw me cry. Letting someone in was a tremendous battle for me. Once I let them in, I became hyper-sensitive to anything I perceived as them thinking of me as weak. Pushing people away was what I did best, although it was never my intention. It was how I had been wired.

I grabbed my travel mug and headed out the door.

It was time to access the place where I had stuffed the painful memories. I was once told that I could take the memories one by one and change the perception I had of them. I couldn't erase what happened, but I could change how it made me feel.

That day, I had a mission to revisit the places where painful memories took place. Followed by the places where both good and bad memories existed. The first stop was the mysterious building with a broken-down fence around it. I believed that this was a place where horrible children like me went, but I didn't know if what I remembered was real.

When I pulled up to the building, I remember thinking that it didn't look as big as I envisioned. It always amazed me how small something looked when you confronted it. The tall fence that seemed so strong and impossible to escape now looked weak and broken down. The building had fallen apart, and trees were growing where the flat roof used to be.

I got out of the car and stood in the spot Mother used to make me kneel and beg to her. I could see her leaning against the truck and drinking her beer. But knowing she could have never left me here took away her power.

I had always wondered what the building was, so I researched the location and found out the building was never a detention center for kids. The building served as a holding center for people with severe mental illnesses who had committed violent crimes and were awaiting trial. My cousin and I once overheard his mother talking to her snotty friends about her brother. He had severe mental illness and ended up in a mental ward after trying to attack a teacher with scissors. The building was where he'd been held. I never heard what became of him, and I had no clue why my mother chose this place to torment me.

I remembered the times she brought me here and how I felt hated, so small, and wished I had never been born. Often, I prayed when no one was around and asked God to take me from this world. Because being here only brought me pain and sadness. I didn't want to be alive. After Grandma died, I asked him to let me go with her.

He didn't, but sweet Rose used to tell me, "Sometimes it's unanswered prayers that lead us to where we need to be. You have a purpose here. Just open your heart, and you will find the answers."

On that day, I stood in front of the building where my mother once tortured my soul. I was dragged out there in the middle of the night to satisfy my mother's sick desire to make me believe I was a bad kid who no one would ever love. That place once represented darkness, where I would rot if I did not conform and obey. So many hours, I begged...

And prayed to be who my mother wanted me to be, so I wouldn't have to go.

It was just a game to her.

One that was detrimental to me.

†

I stopped at a restaurant that was down the street from my grandparent's house.

It was one of my grandpa's favorite places. I walked in the door and requested the booth. Not much had changed. It still had the same booth seats, a faded red with a lot of wear. The tables were still the same, too, a retro 70's style.

The only thing missing was the little jukeboxes on top of the tables. We would sit there for hours while Grandpa visited with his friends. They had the best apple pie in town, my grandpa used to tell me. As a kid, I liked their home fries the best.

After lunch, I headed to my grandparent's place to walk around. When I pulled into the yard, it surprised me to see that everything seemed the same, even though no one lived there. All the flower beds looked like they did the last time I was there. An old ceramic lighthouse still stood, but the color had faded from years in the sun. The stone pots Grandma loved so much were still there but had seen better days.

I went into the garage first, where my grandpa had stored the old cars that he had refinished over the years. I had memories of my cousin, Brandon, and spending hours in this garage helping Grandpa. Sometimes we would sit in the car for hours just talking. I remembered a specific incident at a family reunion my grandparents had hosted.

My mother was drunk as usual and started calling me names in front of everyone. I was so embarrassed, so I ran out to the garage and hid in one of Grandpa's cars. About ten minutes later, my cousin found me and jumped in the car with me.

"Sammie, I'm sorry your mother did that to you."

"It's okay, I really don't want to be in there anymore," I said.

"It isn't your fault she's like that, Sammie. I'll stay with you," he said.

We started talking about Grandpa's cars that he had gotten a couple of weeks earlier. We decided to check them out in the other garage while the adults did their thing.

Brandon always tried to protect me and said things to me that made me feel better. We never talked about the things that happened. He just found ways to distract me and make me smile. I hadn't thought about the times we spent hanging in the garage for a long time.

It looked the same, minus the cars that my grandfather restored and collected, and like everything else, it appeared smaller to me. I walked toward the back, where we used to spend hours putting small engines together. Mostly, I watched and fetched the lemonade when we got thirsty. I smiled when I thought about all the times I spent there with my grandparents.

After a few minutes, I locked the garage and headed toward the house. As I walked up the steps that led into the house, I remembered when Grandma would open the door and greet me. We were always happy to see each other. Some of the only happy memories I had from childhood came from my time in that house with my grandparents.

I walked into the kitchen. The first thing I saw was the old porcelain sink and metal cabinet. When Grandpa remodeled the house, he left it there because Grandma loved that old sink. I recalled Grandma in her apron, baking her bread and preparing meals for Grandpa and me. She always did it with a smile, and sometimes she would sing, depending on how much wine she had.

I walked through the rest of the house, occasionally stopping to take in the view. The pink bathtub was still in the upstairs bathroom. I used to love taking a bubble bath there. The bedroom where I slept when I stayed looked the same. I sat on the bed and looked around. There was the same nightstand next to the bed. My grandma used to put my favorite treat on that nightstand with a glass of water.

I spent the next couple of hours taking it all in, lying on the bed in my grandparents' room, reminiscing about the times I spent with them. I could still smell Grandpa's favorite cologne when I closed my eyes. This space was safe and the only place I felt love. I sat up suddenly as a thought came to me.

That was what we needed to do with my grandparents' property. We needed to build a haven for young women and their children. I locked up and headed home. I couldn't wait to tell Zoë about my idea.

†

I walked into the house. I sat my things on the bar and remembered snapping at Zoë that morning, so before anything, I needed to apologize. Stepping lightly, I headed toward the living room just in case she was asleep.

Zoë was sitting on the couch. She looked at me when I sat down by her feet.

"Hey you, how are you feeling?" I asked.

"Like I got punched in the fucking head," she said.

"Do you need me to get you anything, ice, ibuprofen, a drink?"

"No, I'm good, thank you," she replied.

"I'm so sorry, Zoë, for snapping at you this morning. It wasn't right or fair to you." I looked at her. "You know, I just don't want you to see me as weak."

"You know I'm gonna forgive you, but it gets old." She paused and looked at me. "I'm going to tell you again. What you see as weak, I see as being human. Letting someone in, sharing, and letting go through tears is not being weak. It's being vulnerable with someone you can trust. I'm here in your corner, Sammie, and sometimes you sucker punch me. I know why you put up walls, but I wish you could see you don't need to with me."

"Zoë, trust me, I understand. It frustrates me too. I'm so grateful to have you in my life." I looked at her. "I want to give you that. I do."

Understanding why I did that wasn't easy, especially when I couldn't even wrap my mind around some of my reactions. But Zoë was such an amazing person. I knew I was lucky to have her in my life, but fear kept me in a space where knee-jerk responses and withdrawal happened.

"So, tell me about your day," Zoë said.

I filled her in on the visit to the old building and how different it looked and felt. We talked about the little restaurant where I had lunch and how much it looked the same as when I was a kid. I explained to her how being in the house made me feel.

"When I talked to my grandpa's friend last week, I let him know that my only interest was in the house and outbuilding. I d want all that property. But it came to me when I laid on my grandparents' bed and thought about how safe I always felt there..." I paused. "I want to use that property to build a community for young women who are victims of abuse and domestic violence. A place where they can heal and rebuild their confidence. There are one hundred eighty acres there. Zoë, we could make an entire community that would be a haven for people transitioning from an abusive world to a world where they matter." I talked fast as I told her what I wanted to do.

"Sammie, it's a brilliant idea, and I know your grandparents would be so proud. They would love what you have planned for the property.

"I think so, too."

CHAPTER TWELVE

Confession

Zoë was flying back from New Mexico. She had flown home the week before to spend some time at her office, and to wrap up a couple of projects. She started her company right after college, from the ground up, growing her clientele through hard work. She put the people who were chosen for her team through a very extensive process to ensure that they were the right fit. Not everyone was a fan, but she didn't care. She came to the table with a lot of experience and was respected for her no-nonsense ways. It always amazed me how effortlessly she ran not one but two companies from wherever she was.

We had a meeting scheduled with an architect the afternoon of her return to talk about the plans for my grandparents' property. I remember being so excited about the project and happy that Zoë would be a part of it, too.

I met with Frank the week before to talk about my idea of the property. At one point, I looked at him and saw a tear or two. He thought it was a great idea and said, "Sammie, your grandparents would be so proud."

I smiled at him. "They're leaving the house, barn, and garage. We're going to use them, but we want to maintain the original look if possible. The plan is to build housing for the girls and classrooms. There will be horses and other animals, plus gardens of all kinds because they're therapeutic. We have many more plans as well. Some of the best experts will be involved with the project."

"I love the idea, Sammie, and look forward to seeing it become everything you dream of it being."

"Thank you, Frank."

†

I picked Zoë up from the airport, and we headed to our meeting with the architect and contractors. I sat back and watched in amazement as Zoë took control of the meeting. She knew what I wanted for this project. We'd spent hours talking about the mission and the end goals of the program. I saw the frustration on her face when she realized that neither of these men had come prepared.

"Have you been to the property?" Zoë asked the contractor.

"No, we haven't been out there yet," he said.

"Oh really, do you mind telling me why you haven't gone to the property?"

"We've been really busy," he said.

"Hmm, maybe too busy for this project?"

"No, ma'am, we will make time."

"Do you have a site plan draft with you?" she asked the architect.

"No, but I can email it to you," he said.

"No, I don't need it." She pointed at the contractor and said, "He does."

"Please email him an aerial, too," I said.

"I emailed a copy of the aerial to all of you last week."

"I didn't see it," the contractor said.

"How do you know you even want the job if you haven't seen the site or gotten an aerial of it?" Zoë asked.

"We will get that done this week," he stated.

"Well, we're just wasting everyone's time here today. We're busy, too." Zoë stood up. "When you have the necessary items that we need to start planning, let me know. If I haven't found another architect and contractor by then, I'll give you another chance." She looked at me, and I stood up. We walked out of the meeting room. There was dead silence.

We got into the hall, and Zoë started laughing. "I left those losers with their mouths hanging open. If they think that I'm going to use them just because of their name, they're wrong. I can't work with incompetence."

"Well, have you got someone else in mind?"

"Yes, we have a meeting next week with the architect I've worked with on some big projects. He has an extensive portfolio, and he listens to your vision and can transform it from your mind to the paper. He's a brilliant professional that makes these small-town bozos look pathetic. I think you'll be much happier with him and the contractors he brings with him."

"I trust you with that decision. We don't need bozos on the job." We both laughed.

"Let's get out of here!" she said.

We stopped by this little Mexican restaurant that was on the way home. When we walked in, the amazing smell of authentic Mexican food woke my senses and my stomach even more! We followed the hostess to the back of the restaurant to a big booth. The music that came from the speakers added to the authenticity of our surroundings. I sat across the table from Zoë and thought about the feelings I had for her. They'd started to go past the friendship we had. I loved her more than anyone else, but I couldn't let myself fall in love and risk losing her because of my giant fears. She was beyond amazing, but sometimes it seemed like she was too good to be true. I never acted on my feelings, but sometimes I felt Zoë look at me in a way that made it seem like she was into me, but I was too scared to take the chance.

I ordered a drink to calm my nerves. We talked more about the project and the upcoming meetings we had scheduled. We hoped to break ground as soon as the ground thawed, perhaps right before the spring, and be finished by the summer of 2018.

The food came, and it looked and smelled so good. It sizzled in the pan as the waiter set it in front of me. I loved fajitas. Zoë had chicken enchiladas with rice and beans, which looked good, too. We both ate until we were so stuffed, I felt bloated from eating too much.

As we walked to the car, I tossed Zoë my keys. "Will you drive, please?"

"You tipsy?" She laughed.

"Just a bit from that second margarita, but I'm good. Driving, especially in this area, is not worth the risk for me.

"You can count on me. I would love to drive," she said.

When we got home, I changed into some big comfy pants because my jeans were too tight from my bloated stomach. I returned to the kitchen and made two glasses of raspberry tea. It was only 6:30, but it felt much later. Sleep wasn't always easy because shutting my mind off was sometimes impossible.

Zoë walked out to the kitchen, and she had also changed into baggy pants.

"I feel so much better now that I'm out of those jeans," she said.

"Me too. I ate entirely too much!" I handed her a glass of tea.

"Oh, gosh, me too. Thank you for the tea."

We headed to our normal hang-out in the living room, each taking an end of the couch.

"So, how's the board recruitment coming along, Sammie?"

"It's coming along well. We have a diverse group of members ready to invest their time in the mission."

"Outstanding! And the mission statement?"

"I finished the draft and will present it at the first board meeting next week for review. They'll be voting on officers and reviewing the by-laws and policies. Plus, we will be taking suggestions for a name."

"Care to share?"

I pulled up the draft on my phone and read it to her.

"Wow, impressive. You're making this happen, Sammie!" She smiled at me and took my hand. "I'm so proud of you."

Compliments were hard for me to receive. It was awkward, and I never knew what to say. I looked down at Zoë's hand holding mine. Her grip felt safe. When I looked up, our eyes met. The way she looked at me made me feel strange. I didn't want to move. I felt this weakness come over me, and it scared me. My thoughts were all over the place. *What was love supposed to feel like? Was this it?* Our hands intertwined so naturally, they fit like it was meant to be.

After a minute, I set my phone down on the couch and said, "Geez, this tea is going straight through. I'll be right back."

"No worries, old lady."

"Hush!" I stood up.

I wasn't gone for more than a couple of minutes, but when I returned, the mood in the room had changed drastically. I sat on the couch and looked at Zoë. She looked pissed.

"Zoë, what's wrong?" I asked.

She pointed at my phone. "You missed a call."

I picked up my phone and looked. There was a missed call from Natalie, my ex-girlfriend. I had no idea why she'd be calling.

"You need me to leave the room so you can call her back?" she asked.

"Fuck no, why would I want to call her back?"

She shrugged her shoulders. "Maybe it's important, or she needs you."

"Really, Zoë? This is what you want to do?" I asked.

"Well, why the hell would she have your number? After you told me the things she said to you, I don't understand why she would have the privilege of having your number."

"I guess I just didn't block her. She doesn't make a habit of calling."

"You have some unresolved feelings when it comes to that toxic girl."

"No, I don't. That is bullshit."

"Well, the way you talk about her, you still have feelings."

"That's exactly why I don't open up to people. My drunk ass had to bring up stupid shit with you that doesn't even matter anymore." *What the fuck was it I said to her, and why would that conversation even come up between us?* "Look. Zoë, I honestly don't remember talking to you about her. I have no feelings left for her now, nor will I ever; she makes me sick, to be honest. My desire for peace has led me to speak with her occasionally about things that didn't involve me but focused on what I could do for her. I let her know I had no time, and that was the last time we spoke." Zoë got a blank stare from me. "I don't know why she's calling, and I don't care."

"Well, that girl shouldn't have any access to you after what she did and said. Hell, what she did ranks up there with your mother. It was wrong, and she doesn't deserve to be in your life for even a minute. It feels like you can't let her go, and that's stopping you from living your best life. I don't want to seem like some overbearing, jealous person, but I can't stand that woman or the things she has done to you. If you still want her in your life, I won't stand in your way, but I can't be around to watch you get sucked back in and destroyed by her."

"What the fuck, Zoë." I started to stand up, and she grabbed my hand. I pulled it away. "No, I can't believe you think for a minute I would take her back. I've let you in. You know damn well I don't want her in my life. Please don't make me regret telling you about the things that happened. I trust you with my thoughts. Throwing them back at me is not fair."

"I'm not throwing anything at you. I just don't understand how she still has a right to be in your life. Fuck, I've had to fight sometimes to be here with you, and I'm the one who one hundred persent has your back. I love you, Sammie, but I can't fight for a place in your life anymore. I've sat back and watched her break your heart and treat you like a second-class citizen. I've given you space and my friendship even though my love for you goes beyond that. Natalie nearly destroyed you and she still gets access to you."

"Oh my God, Zoë, no she does not," I screamed.

"That is why you can't have a healthy relationship. Too much baggage," she yelled back.

"I can't with you." I grabbed my keys off the coffee table and stood up. Trying to compose myself before I turned to look at Zoë. "I'm done with this conversation. I've told you how I feel about her, but apparently, it wasn't good enough."

"So, you're going to leave in the middle of the conversation?"

"You mean a conversation where you tell me how I feel? Because what you said is not true. I have no feelings for her. She isn't the person I want to be with." I paused. "I just need to go clear my head so I don't say something stupid."

Zoë quickly stood up. "You know what, Sam?" She walked toward the kitchen. "Save yourself the trouble. I thought being here while you work on your book was the right thing to do. I want what is best for you because I love you, but you don't need me here. I've never been and will never be your first choice."

"That's not true, Zoë."

"But it is, Sammie, and has been that way since that bitch came into your life."

"She is not in my life anymore, Zoë."

"So that's why you want me here now, Sammie?"

"No, that's not why. I know what I did wasn't right and I'm sorry."

She turned to look at me. "I'm going to go home for a while. There are things to wrap up in New Mexico. I need to take time to reflect on some things." She walked toward her room.

"Zoë."

She kept walking.

I should've ran after her and told her how I felt, but I was worried she'd think I was just saying it to keep her from leaving. The truth was, she had been standing on the sideline for a lot of years, and I knew that. It wasn't fair to her. Letting her go was the best for now.

I walked out the front door because being there when she left would only make it harder. I wanted to tell her how I felt. That was what I had intended for the evening. One moment in time changed everything, just a stupid phone call. Zoë was right. Natalie didn't deserve a place in my life and never really did.

Natalie knew the weekend that we got together that I was going out of town with Zoë, and that I was starting to develop feelings for her. I had confessed that to Natalie a few days earlier. She knew what she was doing, and I fell right into her game. She never really loved me. Her intention was to keep me from being happy with someone else. I felt like I was part of some game she was playing. Zoë had every reason not to speak to me again, but she had never turned her back on me.

She was the one that I loved, but I thought it was too late.

I drove around for a while until I got to the beach. I parked and sat in my car. It was almost dark, the time of day when my PTSD was triggered easily, and walking on the beach alone would not be ideal. Every sound in the dark caused my heart to race, and my mind would follow right behind it. The things that existed in the darkness were my biggest fears.

I turned the music on just loud enough to keep it from being silent and watched the sun set over the lake and reflected on the things said. Zoë holding my words against me didn't piss me off as much as me drinking and saying too much. I sat there for a long time, trying to recall what I had said, and wondered why Natalie would be a part of the conversation. I knew how Zoë felt about her.

I decided it was time to head back to the house. Walking into the house brought the reality of the situation to a painful awareness. There was no music playing in the background or Zoë to greet me. I was so sad that she had left, so mad at myself for fucking things up again. My destination was my room, where I planned to have a pity party and had come prepared with a bottle of wine, a corkscrew, and a glass. I screwed up every chance I got at having someone love me. *Why was I like that?* I finished the bottle of wine and passed out. I didn't want to feel anymore.

†

It was several days before I heard from Zoë. She didn't respond to my text. I knew she needed space, but I regretted not telling her how I felt before letting her walk out that door. My fear of rejection was so over the top that I failed to communicate my feelings.

The situation made me feel uneasy. I had no idea what she was thinking. I needed to hike and reboot. After changing clothes, I made my way to my favorite hiking trail. It was about two miles round trip, but a great workout for the mind and body. I missed my hiking buddy, Bella. Things had become so busy that I couldn't give her all the attention she needed. I had sent her home with Zoë the last time she went home. Bella stayed with Brandon and his family until I got back.

I made it to the bottom of the stairs and continued to walk along the path that was lined with trees on both sides. Suddenly, the trees ended, and I was on a secluded beach. The rock bluffs along the shoreline were beautiful. Driftwood lined the beach, and in the distance, I could see the boats pushing through the waves. I sat on a rock. The wind was a bit brisk on this fall afternoon, but the view was worth it. I looked up to the top of the cliff and realized that I would have quite a climb on the way back! A good reason to take a break.

I looked at my phone. Still nothing from Zoë. Maybe I should've just told her. I wanted to tell her in person, but everything had gone wrong since Natalie's call. I composed a message.

Zoë, I'm sorry about what happened the other night. It is not what I had planned for our evening, and I'm disappointed in myself for not telling you how I felt. You are the person I trust with my thoughts, and my life. It is you that is always in my heart and my thoughts. Sometimes I'm scared of the way I feel for you, and I push those feelings away. I'm sorry that I made loving me so hard. I regret not being honest about my feelings.

I pushed the send button. There was no going back. I just hoped it wasn't too late.

CHAPTER THIRTEEN

Natalie

Fall 2010

Dating.

I wasn't sure there was anything that compared to the stress that came from dating. Meeting people had always been difficult for me. The beginning was just awkward and seemed to be where I stumbled the most. I tried the online dating thing because that was the easier way to meet people. However, there was a good chance the person on the other side of the computer had hairy legs and a penis. If you did click with someone the first meeting was comparable to torture. The anticipation caused great anxiety.

It didn't take me long to pick up on the signs of a fake profile. If it looked too good to be true, then it was too good to be true. I had a lot of stories but no connections. There were opportunities for hookups and threesomes, but nothing ever came of my time of online dating. It was a fast-paced ride that made me nauseated, so I jumped off and left that world alone.

Life went on. I spent the spring hiking with a group I met through friends. We frequently hiked new trails and had lots of laughs along the way. I met Zoë then, she was part of our group. I liked her from the start, but I was quite sure she wouldn't look at me twice. She was genuinely nice and always made a point of talking to me when we saw each other out, but I knew it would never go beyond that. Everyone knew that Zoë Barro could have anyone she wanted in the room. Why would she want me?

I spent the summer camping, rafting, and hanging out at the local pub. Life was great. I had a job I loved and great coworkers. Our circle was tight and a safe place to be. We gathered at one house, grilled up a bunch of food, and hung out by the pool. Time passed quickly, and soon fall was in the air, my favorite time of the year.

The girls at work invited me to their annual Halloween party. I wasn't sure it was something I wanted to do. I dodged many invites throughout the years. Large group events were not my thing at all, but part of being in journalism was being social, so I would do what was prescribed by society.

I was dressed as a pirate, with a white Gia Monae Blouse, a black laced-up front vest, black pirate pants, and laced-up black boots. I found a cool pirate's hat at this huge

Strength Within

Halloween store in Albuquerque. When I looked in the mirror, a feeling of anxiety followed. There was a part of me that entertained the thought of calling my coworker to tell her I couldn't make it because something came up. I felt awkward in my own skin.

The other part of me pushed through the thoughts and felt excited. I pulled up to the house where the party was being hosted, and it was an enormous home, and there were so many cars! I heard someone say my name. I turned around and saw Zoë walking toward me.

"Hey Zoë," I said.

"Hello, I'm so glad to see a familiar face!"

"Me too!"

"There are a lot of fucking people here," Zoë said.

"Right. I'm glad to have you here to walk in with me," I said.

"Yes, me too."

As we entered the doorway, there were people everywhere. We saw this hallway, and Zoe said, "I think that the actual party is in the basement."

We walked down the stairs to this huge open room. The girls from work spotted me and motioned for me to come over. "You're welcome to come with me," I said to Zoë.

"That's all right. I'm going to go in here and get a drink so I can deal with this crazy."

Zoë walked off toward the bar area, and I made my way through the crowd to my friends.

"Hey Sammie, look at you, getting your sexy on," a coworker said.

"Oh, stop it," I said, as my face turned red.

"It's a great costume, Sammie," someone else said.

"Thank you, ladies."

After a little liquid courage, I found my way to the dance floor with my friends. I had never danced in public. But at least it was dark, and no one really saw me in the crowd. A couple of songs in, and I had to go back to my seat. Liz, a coworker and a great friend, said to me, "Hey, wait, I'll go with you. I need a drink!"

We stopped by the bar to grab a fresh drink and then walked back to our table. Just as we sat down, I heard someone say, "Hey, cuz."

"Oh my God, Nat," Liz walked over to a woman with long, curly brown hair. "What the hell, girl? It's been forever." She hugged her.

Liz turned around and introduced me to her cousin Natalie from Texas.

"What the fuck has you here?" she asked Natalie.

"I met someone on the internet and moved here," she said.

"What the fuck?" Liz said.

"Just kidding." She laughed. "I took a job at the university in the nursing department. I'm going to be teaching Clinical Immersion and Clinical Leadership this term."

"Nice, Nat, I'm glad you're here. We're going to need to hang out," Liz said.

"For sure."

Our eyes met, they locked for just a moment, and then we both looked away. I downed my drink quickly. We all headed back to the floor and danced the night away. As I looked around, I saw people from all walks of life laughing and dancing together. The vibe in the room was amazing. I had made it and was surrounded by talented people who made me smile.

My thoughts were derailed when I felt someone dancing close behind me. I turned around, and there was Zoë.

"Hey, you, what are you doing?" I asked.

"Watching that chick over there looking at you," she said. She smiled and pointed at Natalie.

"Hush, Zoë."

We both laughed.

"You want to go get a drink with me?" I asked.

"Of course, let's go."

When we got up to the bar, Zoë said, "By the way, your costume is hot."

I giggled and said, "Well thank you, Zoë. Yours is..." I realized she wasn't wearing a costume.

"Oh yeah, I don't do the dress-up thing," she said. She put her cap on backward and winked at me.

"Well, you look good," I said.

I saw Natalie walking toward us and I smiled.

"What are you all googly eyes about?" She turned around. "Oh, it's that girl again."

"Shhh." I elbowed her.

Natalie stood at the bar next to me. "Can I get a Long Island Iced Tea, please?"

"Damn," Zoë said.

I elbowed her again as Natalie turned toward me and handed me a piece of paper. "Here's my number. I'd love to meet up for lunch sometime soon."

"Oh. Thank you. That would be great." I took the paper from her.

When she walked away, Zoë said to me, "Watch yourself with that one."

"Whatever, Zoë, don't be hating."

"I'm just saying, watch yourself."

†

Natalie and I met for lunch a couple of weeks later and seemed to have an instant connection. The conversation was simple as we talked for hours about music, camping, hiking, and many other things. It seemed like we had a lot in common. It felt like a perfect match. We shared stories about hiking in Colorado and camping in New Mexico. We laughed so hard when she told me about a rafting experience.

"Girl, I thought it was over that day. I told my friend it was because I smoked marijuana with her. After that, I was no good. I thought I saw the biggest snake ever and fell out of the raft."

"In the water with the snake?" I asked.

I couldn't imagine...I felt panicked just at the thought of it.

"I was freaking out and climbed on a rock and froze because everything looked like a snake to me."

"Oh, I get it. I would have done the same thing." I laughed. "So, how did you get off the rock?"

"It turns out we were at a shallow part and the current was slow. We'd planned on stopping just ahead at a bend. My cousin swooped my ass up and put me in his raft for the rest of the way. I have yet to live that down."

"Oh my gosh, that is hilarious. So have you been out since that experience?"

"Yes, I just stay away from the pot, and I'm good." She laughed.

After a brief pause, I said, "I hate for this to come to an end, but I have a late meeting I need to get to pretty soon."

The way she smiled at me at that moment almost felt overwhelming but in a good way. Scary as hell because I didn't know how to process the things I was feeling.

"I would like to see you again, Sammie. Are you busy Friday night?" she asked.

"No, I'd love to hang out with you," I said.

"You want to come to my place?"

"Yes, that would be great. You need me to bring anything?"

"Just you," she said.

I couldn't wait to spend time with her again.

†

I went to hang out with Natalie at her place. The nerves were seriously intense as I drove. The part I hated was the beginning when you don't know that person very well. My flight instinct was trying to turn me around. Just go home. It was so much easier that way.

But I didn't go home. I really liked Natalie and wasn't trying to blow it by not showing up. When I pulled up to her townhouse, my stomach flipped. There was no time to doubt my decision because Natalie came right out the front door as soon as I put my car in park. No time for flight.

As she walked toward my car, I gathered up my keys and phone. I opened the door just as she approached. "Hey, you." I stepped out of the car. "You look great."

"Aww thank you," she said.

I closed the car door, and she grabbed my hand and led me toward the house. After we stepped through the door, she said, "Welcome to my casa."

She grabbed me, started kissing me hard, and I was sure she was trying to deep-throat me with her tongue. The shock factor caused my reaction as my body became tense and the entire scene turned awkward.

"Umm thank you," I said a bit dumbfounded. I was not expecting that at all.

"I didn't mean to make you uncomfortable," Natalie said.

"No, you didn't. I was just surprised, but it's all good. It was nice." It wasn't all good or nice, but what was I gonna say?

The way she looked at me was different after the awkward reaction to her kiss. It seemed I had offended her. I wasn't at all prepared for the kiss, and maybe that made me a little under-experienced. But to be honest, kissing for me tended to be soft and slow, building the tension between us as the passion grew.

I couldn't change my reaction, so I had to let it go.

We spent the rest of the evening talking. Natalie shared with me some of her childhood experiences. Her mother seemed like a bitter woman who hated her life. She told me how her mother would make her wear big tee shirts and told her it was because she was fat.

"My mother always told me I was not going to amount to anything. She made fun of me and told me I had my father's ugly nose and big ears."

"Wow, I'm sorry, Natalie, that's fucked up," I said.

"Yeah, a lot of the things she did were fucked up. My dad left because he couldn't deal with her bullshit anymore. He left me there with my mom, and her anger that came from him leaving. She hated life, and being around her was miserable."

"They don't know how their words play with our heads."

"Yeah, I married the first dickhead that came along because he told me I was pretty and smart. Once he married me, it was nothing but a bunch of bullshit." She rolled her eyes.

"Did he change once you guys got married?" I asked.

"Yup. Have you ever been married, Sam?"

"Oh no. Nope, never married."

"Have you ever dated a man?" she asked.

The questions were getting personal, so my nerves came back.

"No. I haven't ever dated men."

"So, you've always known you were attracted to women?"

"Yes, I was confused about it, but I knew," I said.

"Confused?"

"Yeah, I heard my family and the people from church talking about how it was a sin, and you would go to hell. So, I was afraid for a long time, and I wasn't telling them I liked girls, but an incident put the spotlight on me. The biggest reason I moved here was my aunt didn't want me in her house anymore when she found out."

"Oh, wow."

"Yeah, it is what it is. Sometimes you just need to move on." I paused. "When did you discover you were into women?" I asked.

165

"I've always been curious and acted on it one night with this woman I worked with. It was so good, so much more intimate, and intense. I knew I couldn't go back to men."

She looked at me. When our eyes locked, I felt this pull, and so many things went through my mind. *Should I lean in and kiss her? Tell her that her eyes are beautiful?*

Nothing.

I did nothing because the courage to do so did not exist inside of me. It was impossible to open my mouth and speak about anything I felt. I sat there awkwardly; I didn't want to blow it by saying the wrong thing. But I think not saying anything made it even weirder.

I looked away, and Natalie said, "I make you nervous, it seems."

"It isn't you, Natalie. I don't know why I get so weird. I'm sorry."

"No, don't apologize. You have some walls, and I get that." She looked at me and said, "No worries, okay?"

The conversation went on for another couple of hours. Natalie told me more about her life and stories about her past. I just listened because it kept me from having to talk about myself, and then I crashed at her place because it was so late. The next morning, she was rushing around to go into the office to finish up some paperwork.

"Hey. It was nice hanging out with you, Natalie. I had a good time getting to know more about you."

"Glad I didn't scare you away with my stories," she said.

"Same," I said.

We hugged, and I went on my way.

The next day we were texting back and forth when I got a text that said, *I think you are super cool, and I believe we have a great connection, but I don't think the chemistry is there.*

I wasn't surprised when I read the text. I had made it awkward a few times. Disappointed was what I felt. She checked every box for me, and I was very attracted to her. I just didn't know how to deal with those moments. They brought me so much discomfort. I responded with a text.

Oh, Okay

She texted back, *Can we still be friends? I would love to hang out with you.*

I texted, *Of course, we can be friends.*

I didn't know what to think exactly. How did she know so fast that she didn't feel anything? I shook my head as I looked at the text. I didn't understand women.

†

I remember the way the rejection felt. It was deflating and a blow to my self-confidence. Not that I hadn't spent some time beating myself up for not responding differently the night I spent with her. If I had not reacted awkwardly when she kissed me, maybe she would have felt differently. Maybe it was because she seemed to understand me that I felt such a strong connection with her. I was attracted to her completely, but apparently, the feeling wasn't mutual.

I forced myself to be social as the weeks went by, joining a ladies' group and trying new things like attending events. I even started hosting game nights, cookouts, and pool parties once summer came along. Zoë and I became fast friends. It was always light and fun, with no drama or heavy conversations. We laughed a lot and together tried different

167

things like pickleball and disc golf. Zoë and I would meet up with our group often to try out a new restaurant. I felt safe with Zoë, and the time spent with her was easy. There wasn't much conversation about feelings, but the vibe I got didn't seem to go beyond friendship. I was wrong, but my fear wouldn't allow me to see what was right in front of me.

As I reflected on the time before I met Nat and after she told me she just wanted to be friends, I thought of the times I hung out with the group and Zoë was there. One evening after Nat threw me into the friend zone, Zoë and I went hiking with some of the ladies from our group. We fell behind because we were talking.

Zoë pulled her phone out of her pocket and shook her head when she looked at it.

"Is everything okay?" I asked.

"Yeah, just my ex wanting this table we bought when we were together. We split everything when we separated, but she keeps asking for more. I should've given it all to her!"

"Oh, I'm so glad I don't have to deal with an ex!" I laughed.

"Probably because you block people from getting in."

"What!" I looked at her sideways and asked, "What do you mean?"

"I've been trying to break through your walls, but they're huge! When I asked you to dinner you looked at me like I'd lost my mind. But you sure didn't hesitate when crazy girl asked you to go with her."

"Whatever, you were joking, and you know that."

"No, I don't know that, Sammie. Why can't you accept that I want to take you to dinner because I like you."

"Pfft, you know I'm not your type."

"Whatever, Wilson."

The conversation was getting awkward, so I was happy to see the ladies stopped just ahead of us waiting for us to catch up.

"Come on slackers." One of our friends yelled.

We both laughed and started walking faster. Just like that, the conversation ended.

†

Natalie and I hung out on occasion, and I was grateful for her friendship. However, she didn't get along well others—namely my friends. There was an awkwardness that stood out. Although nothing was mentioned, Natalie's mannerisms spoke for themselves. I would avoid any gatherings when Nat and I spent time together. It was simply better that way.

Zoë and I had planned to go with a group of friends to her family's cabin for an extended weekend. There were hiking trails and beautiful places to kayak along the river. The cabin was tucked away in the woods about two miles from where we would be kayaking. The cabin had a game room with a pool table, dartboards, and shuffleboard. There was a huge hot tub in an outdoor garden area that included an outside fireplace.

I was packing my bag when I heard a knock on the door.

Who was knocking?

I opened the door and there stood Natalie.

"Hey you," I said. I opened the door wider and motioned for her to come in.

She walked in and asked, "What are you doing?"

169

"I'm throwing my bag together for the weekend." I walked toward the laundry area to check on my clothes in the dryer. As I came back through the kitchen, I asked, "You want a drink?"

"You have a bottle of water?"

"Of course."

I went over to the fridge and grabbed a bottle of water and set it on the bar in front of her.

We chatted a bit while I waited for my clothes to finish drying. I got a text from Zoë and smiled. *This woman is nuts. I don't know if she will ever pick out something to wear much less enough for two days.* She was referring to her roommate who was a girly girl according to Zoë.

I saw Natalie's lip curl up out of the corner of my eye when I laughed at Zoë's text.

"What time are you supposed to leave?" she asked.

I paused for a moment as I contemplated her question.

Supposed to leave?

"We're meeting up at Zoë's place at four, then we're all going to ride together."

"Oh cool," she said.

I could tell that was not a sincere "oh cool." She had asked the week before if I wanted to go to a concert with her because she had an extra ticket. I told her I was going with Zoë and a group of friends on this trip. Her response had been, "Wouldn't you rather hang out with me?" I had laughed. She was dating someone, so I assumed she was just joking.

I grabbed the clothes out of the dryer and headed to my room. "You can come in here, Natalie. I need to finish packing."

She came into the room and sat on the end of the bed while I folded and hung my clothes and finished packing my bag. There was an awkward silence and then Natalie asked, "What are we doing here?"

I looked at her, "Well, I'm putting my laundry up and...."

"No, why are we not together? Dating and enjoying each other's company?"

A nervous giggle came out of nowhere and out of my mouth came, "Well, we decided to be friends when you said we had no chemistry."

"Yeah, I was being stupid."

I turned around and looked at her, "Natalie, you're dating someone."

"We went out twice; I'm not into her," she said.

"What? I thought you said you liked her."

"I wanted you to be jealous like I am of the girl you are seeing," she said.

"I'm not seeing anyone, and I'm not the jealous kind."

"Yes, I find many things about you that are incredibly attractive. You're a good woman. You have this incredible heart, and I don't want to lose a chance with you just because I'm scared," Natalie said.

"Wow." That was the only word I could find at that moment.

"Have you changed your mind about me?" she asked.

"Well, to be honest, I don't understand why now?"

"Because I could lose you to someone else if I don't speak up."

"Why today when you know I'm getting ready to go with my friends?"

"I didn't want to wait any longer. It has nothing to do with your trip. I've wasted enough time," she said.

She walked up to me, grabbed my hand, and brought her face close to mine until our foreheads touched. Her words were soft, "I'm into you, just afraid of these feelings because they differ from what I know." She kissed me, hugged me tight, and then whispered in my ear, "Please stay with me this weekend. I need you here with me."

CHAPTER FOURTEEN

Is This Love?

I regret not saying no when Natalie asked me to stay with her that weekend. Looking back on it, I should've known it was all just a game. Something inside of me wanted to believe her when she told me she was just scared.

Scared, I could understand.

Why I ignored all the red flags that surrounded Natalie was still a question I asked myself. Maybe it was because I saw something in her eyes in the beginning—at least I thought I did. When she told me she didn't feel a connection, I pushed my feelings aside. That was where I should've left them, but love was indeed blind. I just wanted to be loved.

173

"Sammie, please stay with me." Did she know what those words would do to me?

"So, Natalie, what has changed?" I asked. I needed to know why she suddenly wanted me.

"I realized I was looking for you in everyone I dated. You're smart, beautiful, and have an amazing heart. I'd be stupid to ignore the feelings and let someone else have you. So please come home with me and let me show you how I feel," she said.

Let someone else have you. Those words should've been a big old red flag. The other was the fact she came over right before I was supposed to leave for a weekend with Zoë and friends to tell me she wanted to be with me.

I remember feeling so conflicted, hoping my friends wouldn't hate me forever, especially Zoë. She was going to be so mad. But at that moment, I was thinking with my heart and not my head.

I ended up texting her, *Hey Zoë, please don't hate me! Something has come up last minute, and I'm going to have to cancel for the weekend. Will explain later. I hope you have a great time. Love you!*

She didn't respond, and I wasn't surprised. I knew she was mad. How could I blame her? What I did was pretty fucked up.

†

The weekend with Natalie was amazing. As I reflect on that time, I try to remember why it felt that way. Maybe it was a feeling of being desired by someone. There were intense emotions that intertwined us. Tender moments within each other's arms that felt overwhelmingly safe. My body reacted to her touch in ways I had never experienced. When I entered that unknown space, I had no clue how to navigate my feelings. I reminded myself not to let fear stop me from experiencing the love I wanted so badly. This love I would do anything for...

I remember for the next few weeks I walked on cloud nine. The feelings were intense, and, for the first time, I thought I had found love—my person. Nat and I spent a lot of time together. It was good, relaxing, and we got closer as every moment passed. We talked more about life and our demons from the past. She wanted to know it all. Nat told me she wanted to be there for me and with me through every storm. It was such a good feeling to have someone into me as much as I was into them. Natalie greeted me every morning with a sweet text. We texted all day long about everything and anything, each text bringing a smile to my face.

It was a Friday night, and I headed to Natalie's to cook dinner for us. She answered the door and, seeing her took my breath away. She looked amazing, and the smile on her face made my heart feel warm. I walked in and put the bags on the counter. Natalie gently grabbed my arm, turned me around, and passionately kissed me.

"Well, hello," I said.

"Hey, babe."

I hugged her and said, "I love you."

"I love you, too." She stepped back and asked, "So, what's for dinner?"

I pulled out a bottle of red wine. "Well, I thought we would start with this."

175

"Mm, I'll get us some glasses." She gave me another kiss and grabbed the wine.

"I'd put that in the freezer for a minute," I said.

"I got this. Not my first bottle of wine," she said in a defensive tone.

"Oh hey, I didn't mean anything by that, Nat," I said.

"It's cool."

"Okay." I turned my attention to the food. I made Monterey chicken and served it with a baked potato and a cobb salad I'd made earlier. After making plates for both of us, I walked to the table and placed Nat's plate in front of her and then set mine down.

"Oh my God, Sam, it looks fucking amazing," she said.

"I hope you like it."

Apparently, she did because she posted pictures on social media with a declaration of, "*My girlfriend can fucking cook.*"

Although I used social media, it was mostly for marketing my work. My personal life remained undisclosed, and I never updated my relationship status. I didn't give it much thought because the people in my life knew what was going on.

While in a meeting one day, a notification popped up saying that Nat had tagged me in a post. It was a picture of us at dinner at one of our favorite places. I smiled and set the phone down, then continued with my day. Later, I noticed I didn't have any texts from her. This was not normal. I sent her a text before I got in my car to drive home.

Hey Nat, I had meetings all day. I hope your day has been as amazing as you are. I love you and look forward to seeing you tonight.

No text from Nat yet. Something was going on, and I couldn't help but be worried. Not a day went by without Nat texting me at least once an hour, and it was beyond odd that I hadn't heard from her. I sent her another text, *Hey Nat, I'm worried because I haven't heard from you. I hope all is well. Please let me know if you are okay.*

Around thirty minutes later, I got a text from her that said, *I didn't mean to make you worry. I'm okay. But I'm not feeling up to company tonight. I'm really tired. I'll talk to you later.*

She wasn't feeling up to company... That was strange. I set the phone down and grabbed my laptop and a glass of wine. I had plenty of work to keep me busy, starting with all the emails that came in that day.

A few minutes later, the door opened, and I heard, "Oh shit, Amber, our long-lost roommate has shown up."

"Shut up, Dave," I said.

He walked over to hug me.

He laughed and said, "Good to see you, Sam."

"Same," I said.

Amber walked over and hugged me, then she sat down. "So, what are you doing here, Sammie?"

"I live here!"

"Okay, smartass, you don't come home except to get clothes or whatever." She looked up at me. "You can't tell me that Natalie isn't losing her mind because you aren't there."

"Well, I think she's mad, but I don't know because she isn't talking to me."

"I saw she tagged you in a post today."

"Oh fuck, that's it. I saw it when I was in a meeting, but I didn't comment because I was in a meeting!"

"If she is gonna get mad about that, you need to get the hell away while you still can."

"Nat views social media differently than us. She's a good person and is probably just tired like she said."

Amber rolled her eyes, then she came over and kissed my forehead and said, "Good night, Sammie, I love your silly ass."

"I love you too, Amber."

†

The following day, there was still no good morning text from Nat. I could only speculate on why she was not talking to me. I sent a text anyway.

Good morning, beautiful! Missed seeing you last night. I hope you have an amazing day. Love you.

Nothing. I went on with my day at work, although I found it difficult to focus because my mind kept going back to...*what was she thinking?*

"Hey, Sammie. Are you okay?" I looked up to see a colleague standing in front of my desk.

"Yeah, I'm good."

"The boss is in there yelling about deadlines. Are you done with your piece?" she asked.

"Getting ready to send it to him within the hour."

"Good deal. Well, I hope whatever is going on gets better," she said.

Oh my God, they could tell. The last thing I needed was for people to think I couldn't do my job. I'd worked too hard for my career and the respect of the people I worked with. Before I met Natalie, I considered a job that involved traveling and writing instead of settling in New Mexico. I thought my relationship with Natalie was something different, so I took local assignments. Maybe that had been a mistake.

It was the end of the day, and I headed to my car when I heard a text come in. Once I got in the car, I looked at my phone and saw the text from Nat. *Are you planning to come over tonight?*

I sat and looked at the text for a minute. What the fuck? What kind of random question was that after hours of nothing from her?

I'd love to see you, but of course, that is up to you.

It took her about five minutes to respond.

You're my girlfriend. I just didn't feel well last night. So, let's meet at the restaurant we talked about around six.

I texted back *okay* and then drove home.

†

I met Natalie at the restaurant that she wanted me to try. Her car was in the shop, so a coworker dropped her off. She texted and let me know she got a table. I walked to the booth where she sat, and she looked up briefly, smiled, and went back to her phone.

She was quiet, responding to me in one-word answers. She was on her phone until dinner finally got to the table, and then we ate. I'd never experienced this person before. Nat was normally attentive to me, and we had great conversations. But not today. It was uncomfortable, and it was obvious she wasn't happy with me.

On the way home, she got a call from a friend. She had plenty to talk about with her.

We arrived at her house. She got out of my car and started walking toward her place, still on the phone. I sat there, not sure of what to do. Nat didn't speak a word to me in the car. She stopped before getting to her door and looked at me. She made a waving motion at me, wanting me to come in. There was a big part of me that didn't want to go inside. The way she was acting was not cool. Some days, I wished I didn't love this woman so much.

Once inside, she gave me a one-minute sign and went to her room, still talking to her friend.

I walked to the kitchen bar and sat down on the barstool. A couple of minutes later, I felt a tap on my shoulder. When I turned around, it was Nat's roommate.

"Hey girl, how are you?"

"Good, and you?"

"Headed out to the club! You want something to drink?"

"If you have a bottle of water, that would be great," I said.

"Where is Nat?" he asked.

"In her room, talking to someone on the phone."

"Sammie, you are such a sweet person; not sure she deserves you," he said.

I shook my head. I wasn't about to respond to that.

He walked toward the door as Nat came out of her room.

"Hey, Ryan, you out?" she asked.

"Yup, it's Friday night; gonna hit up the club."

"See ya, be safe," she said.

Nat came up to where I was sitting, took my hand, as she asked, "Come sit with me, please."

We sat on the couch, and what would become a long night was only beginning. So many more red flags I had missed because I only wanted to be loved by someone, and she seemed to be the one that understood me.

The conversation started with her asking me, "So the other day when I posted that picture of us and tagged you in it, why didn't you even acknowledge it?"

"I meant to, but I saw it during a meeting, so I couldn't focus on it."

"You couldn't like it or love it? That literally takes a second."

"Not with this new editor. He's a hothead who expects our undivided attention when he's speaking. After the meeting, he was screaming about deadlines. I never got back to the post to like it."

"Are you trying to hide our relationship?" she asked.

"Of course not. Why would you even say something like that?"

"Because I find it hard to believe that in your position, you have a micromanaging boss."

"Really? So please tell me why I would lie."

She shrugged her shoulders. "Who knows?"

"Look, the people who matter know all about you. Most of the people on my social media are people I haven't seen or spoken to since I left Fredonia. They are there just to see what I'm doing with my life."

"I see. Well, I won't tag you anymore. I don't want to put details out there you don't want people to know." She rolled her eyes as she stood up and walked to the kitchen to get another drink.

"Natalie, that isn't what I am saying. You're twisting my words."

"Twisting your words?" She snapped as she slammed the fridge door. "You know what I think?" she shouted as she walked to the couch and stood over me. "I think you don't want your friend Zoë to know you're happy with me."

"Not everyone is stuck to their social media like you are, Natalie."

"What the fuck. Stuck to my social media? Fuck you, Sammie." She started pacing around the apartment.

I just shook my head.

"You like to poke the fucking bear, don't ya?"

"I'm not sure what that means, but I'm not prepared to continue with this conversation heading in the direction it is."

"Nothing to say about Zoë?"

"She has nothing to do with this, Natalie."

"Sure she does, because you don't want her to see."

"She doesn't even use social media."

"Oh, I'm sure."

"Okay, I think it's time for me to go home," I said as I stood up and walked toward the door.

"If you go home, we're done."

I stopped and stood there with my back to her. She was threatening me with an end.

"If you don't want to be here, then go," she added.

I turned around. "What I don't want, Natalie, is to fight with you, and right now, there is nothing I can say that you'll believe. You apparently know everything I think."

"Okay. Let's stop pushing each other's buttons." She walked up to me and hugged me. "Please stay with me."

I should've left then, but I stayed as she asked.

The rest of the evening was spent analyzing me, and like a bulldozer, she kept ramming into the walls, trying to take them down. But the force was awkward and sometimes overwhelming. The vibe was not something I could embrace, and silent was what I became.

"Why do you shut down like that, Sammie?"

"I don't think that fighting is productive. It makes me uncomfortable."

"You wouldn't fight for me?"

"Yes, of course, I would, but I don't want to fight with you."

"Couples fight sometimes. It's okay."

†

Weeks would pass when everything seemed good. Natalie backed off the attempt to remove all my walls. Although she would remind me that in a healthy relationship, there should be no walls. She didn't like it when I was quiet and would insist there had to be something wrong no matter how many times I told her there wasn't. I'd try to explain to her that sometimes I was just contemplating a piece for work. Other times, I would try to tell her there was nothing on my mind.

"Sammie, I want to know everything about you. I believe we're meant to be together, so we should know everything about each other. You say you love me, but yet you close me out all the time."

183

Although I believed her heart was in the right place, it had become a frequent battle between us. She never believed me when I told her there was nothing on my mind. I'd tell her bits and pieces about my childhood because she wanted to know. Making her happy was one of the most important things to me. I was on cloud nine, looking forward to every text, every word she said, and every song she sent me. I cherished every moment, and I vowed to always give her my all.

†

There were good times when we spent hours just talking and learning more about each other. Looking back, I realize those times were not as often as the difficult moments that came too frequently and sometimes out of nowhere.

One evening I was at Nat's preparing a snack for us, and she came up behind me and whispered in my ear, "Hey baby, I have a surprise for you."

I turned around. "Oh yeah? What is that?"

"Give me a minute, babe. I'll meet you on the patio in just a minute."

"All right." I kissed her and grabbed our drinks and the tray of food.

A couple of minutes later, Nat came out and asked, "Will you try something with me?"

I looked at her, "Well maybe, depends on what you're talking about."

"Please, just trust me, Sammie," she said.

"Okay," I said hesitantly.

She pulled out what looked like a rolled-up cigarette.

"Nat, I love you, but you know I can't stand cigarettes."

She laughed, "It's not a cigarette, baby. It's medical-grade marijuana."

"Oh. I'm not sure...."

"You said you trusted me. Please don't overthink this. It will help you relax."

I just nodded my head. There was no point in arguing with her. She lit the end of the rolled marijuana and inhaled, held it, and then blew out an enormous cloud of smoke. It was my turn, and I'd never smoked, so I just did what she did. I put my lips around the end of it and inhaled, but there was no holding because I started coughing. My lungs rejected it, and I thought I would never stop. She talked me into doing it a couple more times, and suddenly I was laughing and didn't know why.

"How do you feel, babe?" she asked.

"Like my lungs will never be the same, and I've melted into this chair, I'm pretty sure."

She laughed. "I love you."

"I love you, too."

We laughed and talked for hours. She convinced me to smoke more as the night went by, then came the conversation. It seemed the marijuana joint made me feel less inhibited.

Natalie shared a story about the time her mother locked her in a closet for a whole day because she was talking back to her.

"She passed out on the couch and left me in that closet for what seemed like forever. My uncle stopped by to get something out of the garage. He popped into the house and found my mom on the couch. When he woke her up and asked where I was, she was so out of it she couldn't remember. When my uncle said my name, I started yelling." She paused. "He found me and let my mom have it. She never did it again, and I never talked about it."

"Seems our mothers liked their booze!" I said.

It appeared the marijuana gave me the courage to share stories. "My mother used to come home from the bar drunk. Sometimes I would smell the whiskey when she walked into the room. One night she came stumbling in with her friend, Lucy, from up the street. They were in the kitchen. I could hear Mother opening and closing cabinets, then I heard Lucy ask, 'Hey, can I get another glass? This one is dirty. Look, it has a spot on it.' I knew instantly that my life was about to become hell. She came and ripped me out of my room and drug me out to the kitchen."

"In front of her friend?" Nat asked.

"Oh yeah, her friends didn't care. They just sat and watched."

"That's awful. So, what did she make you do?"

"She made me stand there while she prepared the sink for me to do all the dishes in the cabinets."

"All of them?"

"Yes, in hot bleach water. My hands hurt so bad for days between the blisters and sores from the hot water and bleach."

"What? That's cruel, and her friend just sat there?"

"Yes, they drank beer and played cards while I stood there all night, rewashing the dishes repeatedly."

"Wow, your mom was a real monster."

"Yeah."

"Thank you for sharing that with me, Sammie."

"Sure."

I remember feeling exhausted during those times she pushed me to talk. Maybe it was the pot or just talking about my childhood. Disclosing those things was never something I wanted to do, but it was so important to her, so I told her. Putting her needs first was what I did, but letting those walls down didn't make me comfortable. Every time she asked me to talk to her about something from my past, I cringed, and this weird feeling came over me. My subconscious, maybe?

Reflecting on those feelings, I realized something inside of me was trying to get my attention. There was a lot of confusion. How could I love someone so much but never really feel safe in that relationship?

It was not the picture of love I had envisioned, but it was something. Sometimes there was this fear that if I didn't comply with her wishes, I would lose her. The thought devastated me, but by conforming, I was destroying myself.

Was this what love was supposed to feel like?

CHAPTER FIFTEEN

A Broken Heart

A dull ache that can take your breath away. Longing for something that brings you so much pain.

At the beginning of our relationship, I believed Natalie loved me and wanted what was best for me. Every couple goes through the good and bad in their relationship, was what I kept telling myself as the months went by. We both came from a loveless childhood, so there would be challenges, but love would get us through it.

Nat wanted us to have this open and honest relationship, but she made it difficult for it to be that way. She didn't like my friends, so we didn't talk about them. I'd find out as the relationship developed that we were way different. When we first met, it seemed our tastes were similar, but she hated my music and the few TV shows I watched. She didn't like the way I loaded the dishwasher or put the utensils away. As time passed, some things I learned about her shocked me. This wasn't the relationship I had in mind, but I kept hoping that it would get back to how it started.

I couldn't tell her I went to coffee with my friends and that Zoë was part of the group I met up with. Nat would never understand that we talked sometimes, and she had become one of my closest friends. I'd explained to Nat that Zoë and I had always just been friends, but she didn't care. Zoë told me often that she thought Nat was trying to control me, but I put it off as she was just protective and wanted what was best for me.

"You think, Sam?"

That was how that conversation always ended. I was blind.

†

A group of us met up for breakfast one day. Zoë and I lingered and ended up talking for a couple of hours. I was telling her about the night before when Natalie's best friend came over to hang out at the pool.

"I totally felt like a third wheel," I said.

"How do you mean?"

"I don't know. It was uncomfortable. Nat acted like I wasn't there, and her friend kept staring at me. I'm not gonna lie. I think her friend is homophobic."

"What the fuck, Sammie?"

"I'm just saying she doesn't seem happy with Nat's choice. She looks at me with such disgust."

"Screw her, Sammie. You deserve better than that. Why doesn't Natalie say anything to her?"

I laughed. "Because her friend walks on water."

"You're crazy for staying with her, she is so wrong." Zoë shook her head. "I couldn't even get you to go on date with me and I'd give you the world."

I changed the subject.

†

I loved Natalie, but she threatened an ending a lot. She pushed to get a place together and made several appointments to look at different houses. Nat expected me to be there. I couldn't be mad. She put those expectations on me, and I let it happen. I didn't speak up for myself, and that was the only way it would've stopped.

We looked at many houses. Over a two-week period, Natalie had scheduled one appointment after another to look at places. One morning, Natalie informed me we had an eight o'clock appointment that evening to see her "dream" home.

"It's Thursday. I have late meetings, you know that."

"I know that's why I made it for eight, babe."

"It'll be a stretch for me to get there by eight, Nat."

"Sometimes we compromise, Sammie. That was the latest they could show it. You know how long I've waited for this place."

"I'll be there as soon as I can," I said and walked into the kitchen to make my coffee.

"Sam, I want to get a place together. I'm not in this to date forever. I want a life together, all the way, in a place we call ours." She paused and then looked at me. "If you don't want the same, then maybe we aren't meant to be together."

"Why does it go straight to an ending?"

"What the fuck, Sam?"

"Of course, I want the same, Natalie, but I can't just leave the meeting."

"Just get there as soon as possible," she said. She was annoyed.

A couple of weeks later, the moving truck was on the way, and I was taking the big step of getting a place with Natalie. The day I handed over my key to Amber, I had a weird feeling. It felt like I was closing the wrong doors and walking through a door of uncertainty. My friends, especially Zoë, thought I was nuts, and I wasn't certain they weren't right.

†

A group of my friends from college and work, including Nat's cousin and Zoë, invited us to a girls' camping weekend. The mood was great as we prepared our camping gear and all the things that came with it. There was a lot of laughter and affection. We were looking forward to our first camping trip together. She even seemed excited to hang out with the group. It surprised me she wanted to go, to be honest, but her cousin had invited her.

It took years before I could feel safe at a campground. I never told Natalie about Brad and had no intention of doing so because she would turn it into something bigger than it

191

needed to be. She would watch my every move, asking me if I was having anxiety.

We got there, found a spot we liked, and set up our tent. Natalie put everything the way she wanted it, and I just helped as needed. Natalie asked me to tie our hammocks to these specific trees. I set off to do just that. The ladies started arriving, and everyone was getting their tents up and ready for a great weekend. A few of us went off to collect wood. As I walked back toward the pit, I heard a familiar voice. Then I saw the look on Natalie's face and knew without looking that Zoë was there.

Natalie walked up to me. "Did you know that bitch was gonna be here?"

"Wow, Natalie. Name-calling isn't necessary, and she has every right to be here."

"You didn't answer my question," Nat said.

"No, I didn't know who'd be here," I said.

"Uh-huh."

"Natalie, if I knew, I would've told you."

We had a planned hike for the evening while the non-hikers stayed behind to cook. Natalie was one of those who didn't want to hike.

"I suppose you're going to go on the hike with her."

"I'm going on the hike because that is what I like to do with my friends."

She rolled her eyes at me and walked off.

We did a four-mile hike. There was a great incline with a beautiful view of the lake. It was drama-free and nothing but conversation and laughter. We returned to camp in time to help finish cooking and eat dinner.

I got the cold shoulder the rest of the evening. Nat kept to herself, while everyone else was laughing and having a good time. I kept my distance from Zoë, even when Natalie was out of sight. There was no way I was gonna get caught up. At one point, we both ended up in the bathroom, and she asked, "Is your lady pissed because I'm here?"

"Nah, she's good. She's been looking forward to reading in the hammock for days."

"I bet she wasn't planning on seeing me here." She giggled.

"It isn't a game, Zoë. They are your friends, too, and you have a place here. But I'm not trying to play with Nat or have any drama."

"Oh, I know you don't want drama, Sam. That's why I don't understand the reason you want a life with her," she said. "Maybe you like being treated poorly instead of having someone like me who'd always adore you."

The mood turned cold. Zoë walked out of the bathroom.

I returned to the fire and sat down. Although I tried to join in on the laughter, I was aware that my girlfriend wasn't enjoying this trip much. I told the ladies goodnight and crawled into our tent.

A few minutes later, Natalie came into the tent. She sat on the air mattress to remove her shoes and pants. Then she crawled up behind me.

"Why are you not out there with your friends?"

"Because I was ready to go to bed. You know I can't keep up with them." I laughed.

"Right." She paused. "So why didn't you ask me to come to bed with you?"

"I didn't want to bother you. You seemed comfortable."

"You just left me over there in the hammock all fucking night," she said.

"I'm sorry, I wasn't sure what to do. I knew you were mad, but I couldn't just ignore everyone."

"What was I mad about?"

"I don't know, Natalie, not trying to fight with you. I love you."

She rolled over in a huff, and I nearly got thrown off the air mattress. When she stopped, I settled into my spot and fell asleep. Sometime later, I woke up to, "Fuck. I didn't bring my fucking earplugs."

"I'm sorry. I need to go up to the bathroom. You go to sleep, and I'll be back in a few. I'll make sure you're asleep before I lay down."

"Whatever," she snapped.

I walked up to the bathroom, and as I went through the door, I got a whiff of marijuana. Once I got around the corner, I wasn't surprised to see some ladies up there puffing on a big joint.

"What's up, Sammie," one lady said. She tried to hand me the joint.

"No thanks, I'm good right now. Just here to pee," I said.

I walked through a cloud of marijuana smoke.

Their laughter echoed within the concrete walls as the smoke rolled through. Too much time spent there could've led to a contact high as the smoke thickened.

I walked out of the bathroom and nearly went head-on into Zoë, as I let out a scream. She laughed.

"Sorry, I didn't mean to scare you."

"It's okay,"

I walked back to the campsite and sat by the fire pit. There was a small fire still going. I threw a couple more logs into the pit and grabbed a beer. Zoë and her friend, Andie, came and sat by the fire.

"Those girls got that bathroom looking like Cheech and Chong crashed the party," Andie said.

I laughed. "Right. Did you get a contact high, Andie?"

"No, a bit too much alcohol." She giggled.

"Nothing wrong with that," I said.

"Why are you out here and not asleep?" Zoë asked.

"Woke up with a full bladder," I said.

"Whatever, Wilson," Andie said as she slurred her words. "I heard her cussing at you in there."

Omg, please don't let Natalie hear Andie.

I motioned for her to shush. "I think you're hearing things, Andie."

"Nope, she was mad about your snoring," she whispered.

"Okay." I took a drink of my beer. I wasn't going to continue the conversation.

Zoë looked at me and shook her head.

†

A few weeks later, Natalie and I went to a cookout that her best friend's family hosted. I tried to get out of going, but Natalie wasn't having it. It was so uncomfortable the way this woman and her family looked at me. The fake smiles, along with the phony interest and conversations. I told Natalie that her friend didn't like me, and she said, "Oh, it just takes her time to warm up to people."

That day, I confirmed what I'd believed all along. It happened when I'd gone to the bathroom that was near the front door and off the kitchen. Nat was in another area of the house talking to someone she went to school with. I came out of the bathroom just in time to hear, "Natalie needs to break away from that woman because she's not gay, and I'm not sure what's wrong with her." I overheard Nat's friend tell someone else.

Then a male voice said, "Natalie has been smoking pot. She asked me if I wanted to smoke with her. It must be that woman's influence."

"Well, I don't know, but I'm having dinner with her soon. I'm going to talk some sense into her."

"Good luck," the male voice said.

"She'll listen to me. She always does," she said with confidence.

Wow. I knew she didn't like me...

I put on my best poker face and made my way through the kitchen. The male voice was her brother-in-law. They both looked at me—their faces indicative of one's mind screaming...*Oh my God, did she hear us talking shit?*

The cheesy smile, as I walked through, only twisted the metaphorical knife they felt in their gut as they worried themselves sick for the rest of the night.

I never mentioned it to Natalie because I knew she would take her friend's side. Love made me ignorant because that was a huge red flag that I disregarded.

The weeks went by. Some days were better than others. I walked through each day with the best intention. The realization that I was one half of an unhealthy and toxic relationship would get heavy. Hurting Natalie was something

I could never do. I told myself it would get better—she just had a lot on her plate. I tried to love her through it, but at some point, I became numb to it all.

†

The holidays were upon us, our first together as an official couple. I couldn't be more excited about spending the holidays with her. We had dinner one evening with my cousin and his wife. Natalie and Brandon's wife were talking about where Nat wanted to get married and what she wanted us to wear. I looked at Brandon, and he grinned. We had never really talked about marriage, and I wasn't sure how I felt about that with her.

I headed out to work on an assignment for a couple of hours, and Natalie was going to dinner with her best friend. Thankfully, she didn't ask me to go with them because I would rather not be around that woman. I thought about what I overheard her friend tell her brother-in-law and part of me thought about saying something, but I decided it wasn't worth the drama.

I went to bed without another thought about any of it. Anytime Nat went out with her friend, she was out for hours. But when morning came, and she was not in bed, I wasn't sure she had come home. I got dressed and walked out of the bedroom. Nat was asleep on the couch. I thought I must have been snoring again.

One thing that would trigger a fight between Natalie and me was my snoring. She told me I snored so loud it disturbed her sleep. The only way I knew how to remedy the problem was to wait until she fell asleep before I did, with the hope she would not wake up if I snored. That didn't work, either. The incidents were occurring more frequently and became a thorn in my existence. Something I couldn't control and stressed about daily.

"Fuck."

She snatched her pillow and stormed out of the room while yelling.

I followed her and begged her to go back to bed. "I'll sleep on the couch. Don't know why I snore so loud, but I'm sorry that it disturbs you."

"It's probably the fucking anxiety medicine you take," she snapped.

"I'll talk to my doctor and see if there's something else. I'm sorry."

"Fuck, Sammie, I need sleep. Leave me alone."

She stormed back into our room and slammed the door.

Sleep never came to me, as my mind was in overdrive. I ended up working all night. I had an assignment that needed to be completed, anyway.

Natalie walked out of the bedroom. I was sitting at the table, still working.

"Did you sleep?" she asked.

"A bit," I lied.

"Sorry I was so cranky. I just needed sleep."

"I get it. No worries," I said without looking up.

"All right, I love you, Sammie."

"Love you, too."

I'd realized saying that was more of a robotic effort, and I felt numb eighty percent of the time.

†

I grabbed a shower and was getting ready to head out when there was a knock on the door. When I opened it, my neighbor, Tessa, was standing there.

"Hello," I said.

"You alone?" she asked.

"Yes."

"Okay, good. I need to talk to you for a minute." She paused. "Come on, let's go to my place. I don't need your girlfriend showing up."

She grabbed my hand and headed to her house.

"What's up?" I asked, as I sat on her couch.

"What the hell is going on over there? She isn't putting her hands on you, is she?"

"No, she hasn't," I responded.

"My cousin and I were sitting out on the deck last night, and it sounded like someone was getting slammed against the wall," she said.

"Probably just her moving some stuff around."

"Girl, please, I heard her screaming at you a lot."

"I swear she hasn't put her hands on me. There's a hole in the wall in the closet, but I didn't see how it got there."

She rolled her eyes. "You know how it got there. That woman is unhinged for real."

"It's only occasionally when she's exhausted. I'm not always the best with my approach."

"I heard her again last night, girl. My cousin and I were sitting out there again. You know I'm a night owl! My cousin even said something. If we can hear her out in my backyard, she's loud."

"That was my fault. My snoring woke her up, and she was tired."

"I know I didn't just hear you talking crazy. That's no excuse for her to be yelling like that."

I didn't know what to say. It went from me walking on cloud nine to walking around on eggshells. But it didn't change my love for her. I just wanted to make things better, so she would want to love me the way she did in the beginning.

"Listen, girl, I know your heart. You are a brilliant writer and a kind soul. You deserve to be treated way better than that," she said.

"This project just has her worn out. It will get better. I need to talk to my doctor about my medication, too. I think that's what causes my snoring."

"Oh, girl, about that. What was up with her telling you that you need to stick one of those pills under your tongue before you left so you don't have a panic attack in front of everyone?"

"Yeah, my fault for telling her about my anxiety. She is on me about it all the time. Most of the time, I don't feel anxious until she tells me I look that way."

"You deserve way better, sister. I promise you do. You shouldn't have to be screamed at because you snored. That's not normal, and you should be able to talk to her about things without worrying that you will have to eat it later." She shook her head.

"It'll get better; she just had a lot going on. There are more good times than bad," I said.

"If you say so, Sammie. You know I love you, girl."

I stood up. "I better get going. I have a meeting." I hugged her. "I love you, too."

†

The following evening, I was just getting home, and as I walked up to the door, I saw Tessa sitting on her porch. I walked over to her porch and said, "Hello. How are you?"

"Girl, you must have lost your mind coming over here. She sees you here, and your evening is going to be a shit show."

"Whatever, Tessa. Anyway... I'm working on a piece for next week about people who make a difference in our community. I would like to interview you and a couple of your students."

"I'll think about it." Something caught her attention, and then a door slammed at my place.

"Natalie?"

"Yup, I told you," she said.

"I don't know what to say, Tessa. I don't understand."

"Of course, you don't, because you have a big heart, and you're blind to her crazy or something. But you need to open your eyes because that girl is unhinged."

My phone vibrated.

"Speak of the devil," Tessa said.

It was a text from Natalie.

When you're done flirting with the neighbor, I need to talk to you.

"You better go, girl, and she better not do anything stupid," she said.

"It will be fine, Tessa. I'll email you tomorrow about the interviews."

"Okay, sounds good. You take care, girl."

"Of course," I said.

I walked to our house and entered the living area. Natalie was sitting on the couch when I went in. The look on her face made it clear she was pissed off about something. Her eyes shot darts as her nostrils flared.

"I was not flirting with our straight neighbor. I was talking to her about interviewing a couple of her students for the paper."

"I don't give a fuck, Sammie."

"Wow, I'm not going to have a conversation with you right now, Natalie. You're obviously mad, and I refuse to fight with you."

She stood up and started walking toward me, jabbing her finger in the air as she yelled, "You will hear what I have to say."

"Don't come at me like that, Natalie," I warned.

"Oh, fuck off, Sam, I'm done, and I can't believe I wasted so much time with you."

"What the fuck, Natalie?"

"You're broken beyond repair, and I'm not in love with you anymore. I felt sorry for you, so I kept trying to love you. I can't pretend anymore."

I still had my keys in my hand, and I turned around and walked toward the door.

"You have nothing to say?" she asked.

"No."

"You have a month to get your stuff out of here. I've spoken to an attorney, and I'll buy you out of the house."

"I'll let you know when I'll be back for my stuff." I walked out the door and to my car.

Numb. I didn't even know how to react to what had just happened. I got in my car and closed the door. I just sat there with thoughts colliding in my brain.

There was a tap on my window. I looked up, and it was Tessa. I rolled down the window.

"Sammie, you okay?" she asked.

"Yeah...well, I don't know what just happened. I need to go...somewhere."

"You okay to drive?"

"Yeah. I just need to go."

I drove away as I texted Amber, *Are you home?*

Yes

Can I come by, please?

Of course

As I drove over to Amber's place, the tears flowed. I was in shock and wasn't sure why. It had not been pleasant the last few weeks, but I didn't quit the people I loved. I thought she loved me, too, but I was wrong.

As soon as I was at Amber's, I knocked on the door. Amber answered and immediately asked, "Sammie, what's wrong?"

"Have you found a roommate yet?"

"Well, long story, but I had to give them the boot last week. Why?"

"Can I come back?"

"Of course, you can, but what happened?"

"Natalie and I are over; she gave me a month to get out. But I don't want to go back for another day."

"Wait, what?"

"She told me she doesn't love me. I'm broken, and she only stayed with me because she felt sorry for me."

"What the hell? Girl, I know it hurts, but you are going to be better for it." She walked over and hugged me. "When do we need to move your stuff?"

"I'm going to hire movers, but tonight I just want to drink until I can't feel anything."

†

I spent two days in bed. My phone was dead, and I didn't care. I let my boss know I was going to need to take a week to move, so there was no one that I needed to talk to right then. Amber would come to check on me and tell me to get my ass out of bed. I told her I would, eventually. My heart hurt, and nothing made that pain go away, so I slept...for hours until my body hurt.

I had to get up and put myself back together and take care of what I needed to do. The plan was to go pack what I had at that house so the movers could come to get it. I would do the packing while Natalie was at work. I texted her and told her what time, and she acknowledged it. But when I got to the house and tried to disarm the alarm, my code wasn't working. I called the service provider, and they told me the code had been changed a couple days earlier.

I texted Natalie. Why is my code not working?

I just unarmed it. So, you can go in now. Just so you know, most of your stuff is already in the garage, she responded.

I didn't bother to answer. I went out to the garage, and my stuff was all stacked in the corner. My clothes were laid over the boxes and a couple of pieces of furniture. I opened the garage door and started packing the things that were stacked on my furniture. I went room by room to make sure I didn't miss anything. I had just finished in the kitchen and had a handful of stuff that I was taking out to a box in the garage. I saw Natalie's car pull up; she had told me she wouldn't be home until much later.

She walked into the garage. I just kept putting stuff in the box.

"I came by to make sure you could get in, since you didn't respond to my text."

Silence.

I had nothing to say to her. I taped the box and put it on top of the stack.

"Do you need any help?"

"No."

I walked into the house to get the stuff that I had put on the counter in the kitchen. I had only a few more things to box up, and I could get out of there. She followed me around to make sure I didn't take anything of hers. Grabbing the things that were left, I tossed them in a box. I didn't care if anything else of mine was there. I was done.

Without looking at her, I said, "The movers will be here tomorrow morning around eleven. I would appreciate it if you made sure the alarm is off." I picked up the tape. "Oh, and by the way, that service will be transferred to my place on Friday."

"Okay," she said

I walked away.

"Sammie, hold on."

I just stopped in place. I didn't turn around.

She walked up to me. "I didn't mean to hurt you."

"I'm sure," I said.

"I tried to love you, but your broken makes it hard to do so. You need help."

"Not your problem." I started walking away.

"So, this is how it's going to be?" Nat asked.

"How did you think it was going to be?"

"She was right, you know?"

"I don't care who was right, it's over."

She walked in front of me, stopped, and looked at me. "I don't think you understand, Sammie. I'm telling you that your mother was right. I found dishes with spots on them in the cupboards," she said.

Oh my God, I know she did not just say that. I needed to get away from her before I said something I would regret later.

"You aren't the person you pretend to be." Her voice got louder.

I walked toward my car, and she followed.

"You wasted my fucking time. You should warn people about what a fuck up you are so they don't spend time they can't get back. What a fucking disappointment you are! No wonder your mother didn't love you." She was getting louder.

I was opening the door to my car when I heard Tessa say, "Girl, you need to leave her alone and shut your mouth."

"Mind your business," Natalie said to Tessa.

"Girl, you made it my business by being loud and stupid."

"Fuck off," she said as she walked back into the garage and shut the door.

Tessa asked, "You good, Sam?"

"Yeah, I'll see you later, Tessa."

I waved and pulled out of the driveway, ready to be out of there.

The next day, I met the movers. They were fast and had everything loaded in no time. I locked everything up for the last time and put the key in her mailbox.

†

I had missed the red flags; I was blind to the recurring pattern in her previous relationships until it was too late. A euphoric beginning with attentive magical love...little did I know this would be the start of a roller coaster ride that would render me merely a shadow of the person I used to be. She had made me feel safe, and her undying love and support were an unfamiliar experience. She lifted me and made me feel like I mattered, using what I disclosed to her to carefully craft a false safety platform to which she knew I would respond, because I let her past my walls. I had felt lucky. I was grateful to have someone who loved me so much, my soulmate.

But then it all changed; the safe place became toxic, and the cloud became eggshells. The compliments were replaced with criticism and defamation with a direct aim. Silence and tension replaced tender moments. Laughter was replaced with rage-filled outbursts and verbal aggression. There was no way to win with the threat of an ending if I didn't conform.

I became silent and went through the motions—lost myself in conflict and heartbreak.

Discarded...The ending was so cruel. Numb was all I felt.

CHAPTER SIXTEEN

The Haven

2017

Summer quickly turned to fall, and it had been weeks since Zoë left. She went back to New Mexico. I missed her. I admitted I was frustrated that I hadn't told her how I felt right then. There were many times I wanted to pick up the phone and ask her to come back to Wisconsin. Something always stopped me from going there. Maybe it was pride, but most likely, it was my way of thinking that stopped me. A cycle I fought to end because it was exhausting to always battle thoughts and fears.

Zoë had called me out about these fears. Telling me I had allowed them to keep me from living fully. Since the night she left, I had been reflecting on a lot of things. I believed that being in Wisconsin and confronting the things that happened may be exactly what I needed to free myself from the thoughts that had held me back. I wondered if it was too late with Zoë. I thought about the times she had asked me out. I always brushed them off as a joke. Was it possible she really did have feelings beyond friendship for me this whole time?

Zoë had texted me a few times since she left to say hi and tell me about work. She always asked me how the safe-haven project was going. She told me she was wrapping up the projects she had been overseeing while in Wisconsin. However, she had to extend her stay in New Mexico because one of her lead designers was on maternity leave. I missed her so much, but I was grateful that we talked several times a week. I would've given anything for a Zoë hug.

We had been on three-way calls with the architects, and she virtually attended the board meetings via Skype. We used FaceTime to go over the property and building plans. There was laughter, and together, we accomplished so much, but it wasn't the same. The walls between us were back— fears brought them. I had so many things to tell her, but it was too late, and I couldn't do it now.

Hearing about Zoë's ex visiting Albuquerque made me realize it was time to move on. I wondered why she didn't tell me Alex was there. Uncertain of the details, my mind went all over the place with thoughts of what ifs and should haves. I couldn't be mad if they got back together. It was my choice not to speak about my feelings until she had already gone. I wanted so badly to text Zoë and smother her with words of my undying love and affection. But how tacky would that be? It was time for me to let go.

Weeks turned into months since Zoë left. I stayed in Wisconsin for the winter to oversee the Haven project. The owner of the house was happy to extend my lease. The last thing I wanted to do was go back to New Mexico and come face-to-face with Zoë and Alex. I spent the holidays working as much as possible. The weather was frigid, so I didn't spend much time outside. Lexi and Lou insisted I join them for the Holidays.

During down times, I continued the work on my book project, revisiting places from my past where memories had trapped me. Writing helped me process the memories, the things that happened, and how they affected my life. It helped me come to terms with the way I handled things and processed feelings. I realized Zoë was right. I had allowed people and the things that held me back keep me from living life to the fullest.

Sometimes it was hard to know where to start when I was overwhelmed by conflicting feelings. The voices interjected doubt in my every thought. Sometimes the voices won because I was tired of the fight. I wanted to believe that I deserved to be loved by someone like Zoë. Then something would happen that would confirm my doubts and I would give up.

I threw myself into my work, the thing I seemed to do well. The Haven project meant a lot to me and took a lot of my time. Many people would benefit from the programs, and find a safe place for them to heal, recover, and find their independence. There were no other programs like it. The property and the design were one of a kind. It was one hundred and eighty acres dedicated to developing a community where women would feel safe for many years to come.

Our attorney requested a name for our 501(c)(3) certification. We assembled our board and elected officers. Everything was coming together, and we had a lot of great people involved in the project. Folks from all levels of society had come together for a mission. They had put in hours of work that would make the opening day a success.

At one meeting, we were discussing what positions we would need to fill to accomplish our mission. And salaries. As we talked about the administrative positions we felt would be necessary to accomplish our mission, one person kept coming to mind.

"I have someone in mind who I believe is perfect for a position here. She's the young lady I wrote my recent feature story about for the magazine. Right now, she's working on her bachelor's degree. She is so smart, and I think she would be a great addition to our team. I would like for you all to meet her at our next meeting," I said.

"That was an incredible story, and I saw both of you speak at the women's conference in Madison. I believe she is a perfect fit for this organization. She is so inspiring," one member stated.

"She is an amazing young lady. I'll meet with her soon and arrange for her to come to our next meeting if she's interested."

We discussed the progress and what we needed to do before opening day. Our meeting was nearing an end when I said, "Before we leave for the day, I would like to bring up the name, or the choosing of one, specifically for the organization." I paused. "Safe Haven is not available. There's a daycare across town with that name."

"Yes, thank you, Sam, for bringing that up." The chairman paused. "If everyone will send in your name and suggestions to me, I'll compile a list, and we'll vote via email so I can get it to our attorney for the paperwork."

Everyone agreed, and we adjourned the meeting.

†

It had been over two years since Lexi and I met—she had come so far. Our friendship had done the same. She amazed me with her strength and perseverance. While she was finishing inpatient rehabilitation to recover from her physical and mental wounds, she had completed her GED.

She was so kind and beautiful and an inspiration to everyone. She was working on her bachelor's degree in social work. As I sat across the table from Lexi, it was so good to see the sparkle in her eyes. She was excited about the new apartment she found near campus.

"It's four bedrooms and four bathrooms with a huge game room downstairs. There is a hot tub on the lower deck. I can't wait to move in," Lexi said.

"Wow, that sounds great," I said. "What are you going to do with all those rooms?"

"Lou's cousin and her girlfriend are going to move into one room. Lou and I will each have a room, and then Lanie is going to take the other room."

"I'm so happy for you, Lexi."

She smiled at me. "Thank you. I can never thank you enough for all the things you have done for me and for believing in me."

"You made it easy, Lexi." I looked up at her. "You have inspired me."

"Aww thank you." She smiled and said, "So, what did you want to talk to me about?"

"You know the plans I have for my grandparent's property?" I asked.

"Yes, I think that is awesome."

"I would love for you to be involved in the planning." I took a bite of my sandwich and waited for her response.

She looked at me for a moment. "What do you mean?"

"Well, I know you have classes and don't have a lot of time, but I would love to have your input on what programs would empower these young girls. We had a board meeting earlier this week, and I mentioned you. They would like to meet you." I paused.

"Are you serious?" she asked.

"Of course. You would be a brilliant advocate for the people we serve. Full disclosure. They are interested in having you take a position with the agency per my recommendation."

She just looked at me. I suspected her mind was in overdrive. I knew Lexi would do amazing things in any role she took on.

"Would you mind joining me for some meetings with the planning committee and our board?"

She smiled. "Oh my gosh, yes, I would love to, Sam."

"Yes! I was hoping you would."

I reached across the table and took her hand.

"I can't wait to work with you on this. The Haven is going to be life-changing."

"So, is that the name, the Haven?"

"No, the board is voting on a name at the next meeting."

"I look forward to being a part of this amazing project, Sammie," she said.

She squeezed my hand. We talked until they were closing the restaurant. When we walked out to our cars, Lexi asked.

"Sam, I have been wanting to ask all night but wasn't sure if I should or not."

"So, ask me, Lexi. You know you can ask me anything."

"What's up with you and Zoë?"

"Oh.... well, she's in New Mexico wrapping up some projects."

"You two good?"

"Yeah, we're good. She'll be coming up for some meetings," I said.

"I think the two of you are so adorable together. Why aren't you a couple?" she asked.

"Oh, we're just friends."

"That's a shame," she said.

I looked at her and laughed. "You think?"

"Yeah, I do, Sammie."

"Her ex flew into New Mexico a week after she did. I think they are trying to work things out. Zoë was really into Alex, and when she left, it broke her heart."

"I don't know much, Sam, but I see the way you look at each other. You aren't going to just give up, are you?" she asked.

"I'm not sure I know how to do anything else. I made it impossible for her and she stuck around, anyway. When she

left, she told me she was tired of fighting to be in my life. I
don't know where to go from here, especially since Alex is
there. I may be the last thing on her mind."

Lexi opened the door to her car and then turned to me.
"Sam, I know that it's hard to let someone in. It took time for
me to let you in, and there are many people who haven't
even come close. So, I get it, I do, but that girl loves you. I
can tell by the way she looks at you." She reached out to hug
me, and as we embraced, she whispered, "Let her in, my
friend."

She got in her car and drove off. I walked to my car and
got in. I sat there for a moment as I wondered if Lexi was
right about Zoë.

The thing was I had pushed her away for so long that I
feared she might not want to try anymore. I couldn't really
begin to even guess because our conversations were always
about the project. To be honest, that left more room to
overthink everything, and I was too afraid to ask any
questions. Maybe not knowing was better than knowing. Oh,
how I wished there was a way to shut off my mind.

†

It seemed like summer came fast that year after a very
mild winter, allowing the contractors to start early. They had
finished the community's construction ahead of schedule,
however there was still a lot of work to be done before
opening day by early summer. Many finishing touches and
details would need to be wrapped up.

The project had come together so fast. We'd been blessed
with the best team of people. Zoë's architect was amazing

and did exactly as she had said he would. He took my vision, did his magic, and made it a reality. He suggested top-notch contractors. They turned my visions into incredible buildings and functional places for our community.

I took Lexi to the next meeting and introduced her to the board. They offered her the position of Program Director with accommodation that allowed her to complete her degree. She earned that spot without a doubt, and she was an outstanding advocate for the community. As a survivor, she knew better than anyone the needs of the young ladies who would come to our program. When I mentioned to her that she needed to make sure she was not pushing herself too hard, she said, "Staying busy works for me and this will be a great way to start my career. I can manage it, promise."

"There are no doubts in my mind, but don't forget to take time for yourself, too." I paused. "That is so important."

"Like you do, huh?" She giggled.

"Hey now, the last time Zoë was here, I took a ten-day staycation."

"You should take another one soon, with her." She winked at me.

I laughed. "You're crazy!"

Lexi and I walked into the meeting and took a seat. The table soon filled with the board members, contractors, and other people involved in the planning. Zoë was with us via Skype, and her designers were there working on-site. Hearing her voice reminded me of how much I missed her, but I had to focus on the opening day ceremony.

At the last meeting, the board had requested that Lexi and I speak at the event to introduce community members to our organization and our mission. The Department of

Rehabilitation Services would be there to talk about their programs and discuss their involvement.

The day the board announced the name of the organization may have been one of the best days ever. Lexi had no idea what would happen that day and I was super glad to be there with her. It was an honor. We had reached the end of the meeting when the president of our board said, "Before we dismiss for today, we have a legal name for our organization." The group clapped.

"The board voted unanimously for the name to be Lexi's Place."

I heard Lexi gasp and turned to her. She looked completely shocked. Everyone stood and started applauding. Lexi looked like she didn't know what to do.

We all sat back down, and I reached over and took Lexi's hand. "Are you okay with this?" I asked.

"I don't know what to say," she said.

I squeezed her hand.

The president remained standing. "Lexi, we are all honored to have you as part of our organization. When it was time to name this organization, we worked hard to make it happen. We all agreed there was only one name that seemed appropriate. Your strength and compassion inspire all of us. Lexi's Place will encourage many more."

"I don't know what to say. You all really surprised me. I am truly honored. Thank you all so much."

As we wrapped the meeting that day, a board member asked Zoë if she would be at the event, and she replied, "I wouldn't miss it. I will see you all there!"

This weird sensation came over me when I heard her say that. A flutter, or was it my heart jumping? It was difficult for me to process my feelings. They were different. I felt things with Sarah, like little flutters here and there. With Natalie, some moments were unbelievable, and I had never felt those things with anyone else. But with Zoë, it was far more intense. The way it felt when her arms were around me, there was no place I would rather be.

The board president called the meeting, pulling me away from my thoughts.

"Sam, are you okay?" Lexi asked while we gathered our notepads.

"Yes, of course. Just have a lot rolling around in my head in preparation for the opening day ceremony."

"Nothing to do with Zoë coming?" she asked.

I looked at her. "Of course, I want her here. It'll be weird, but I can't focus on that."

"Don't overthink it, Sam."

"Of course, I will," I said with a chuckle.

We walked out to my car and got in. As we were driving back to her place, I said, "Lexi, thank you for all your hard work."

"Thank you for believing in me," she said.

"You make it easy." I smiled at her.

†

Once home, I got some tea and headed to my laptop to do some work on my book. As soon as I sat down, my phone started going off. It was Zoë trying to FaceTime with me. I hated FaceTime, if I was honest, but I answered.

"Hello," I said.

"Hey, you. I miss your face."

"Is that why the FaceTime?" I laughed.

"Yup," she said.

She took a drink of her wine. "So, how are my designers doing?"

"They are doing great work, probably because they have an amazing boss."

"You think?"

"Yeah, I know."

I decided to go for it and ask her about Alex because not knowing was driving me crazy. I couldn't believe she wouldn't have told me by now if they got back together.

"So, I hear Alex is in the city," I said.

"In Milwaukee?" she asked.

"No, there. Why would she be here?"

"Well, why would she be here?" she asked.

"I don't know. I just heard she was in Albuquerque."

"When did you hear that?" she asked.

"Shortly after you returned to New Mexico."

"I heard she was here, too, but I never saw her."

"Oh, I see."

"You thought we were back together? Really?"

"I didn't know."

"You should have asked and saved your mind the trouble. I'm sure you have played out many scenarios. What you need to know, Sammie, is that I wouldn't do that. You would have known. But she isn't my person."

"Good to know."

That was all I could say. I really wished she were in front of me so I could hug her.

I couldn't wait until Zoë returned.

CHAPTER SEVENTEEN

The End?

Early Summer 2018

I walked to the small stage and looked out at the crowd. It was amazing to see how many people came to support our opening day ceremony. The nerves I felt throughout my body gave me a tingling feeling. My knees were a bit wobbly as I made my way across the stage. No matter how many times I spoke in front of people, the nerves never stopped; they just got easier to deal with.

The president of the board introduced me and handed me the mic.

"A new beginning. Everyone deserves a chance to have one. The property we stand on was my late grandparents.

They were two of the most compassionate people I've ever known. They didn't know a stranger and would go above and beyond to help someone. When I learned my grandparents wanted me to have the property, I knew I wanted to turn it into something that could help many individuals. Together with a group of remarkable people, we created Lexi's Place, a multi-service community for women and children. Domestic violence of any kind has a significant impact on our communities. They estimate that one million people in Wisconsin are victims of domestic or sexual violence. That is not okay, and the lack of resources and services only isolates these victims even more. Too many stay in the abusive situation because they can't see a way out. We want to be the light they find that leads them away from a life no one deserves to live. Our mission at Lexi's Place is to provide a safe place for healing and recovery in support of victims of sexual assault and domestic violence. We will strive to help individuals gain the strength to create new beginnings. We appreciate all your support and for showing up to help us celebrate the opening of Lexi's Place. With that being said, I would like to introduce our board of directors and our administrative staff, who have worked endlessly to make today happen. After introductions, we will begin the tours."

After I introduced everyone and people started making their way toward their groups, Zoë walked up to me and asked, "Do you have a minute?"

"Of course, I was going to go to the office. Walk with me?"

"Yes, of course."

We went up to the house that used to be my grandparents'. It was three floors, and we had converted it into offices, with a daycare on the lower level for staff and our volunteers' children. We walked into the office, and I said, "It's good to see you in person, Zoë. I've missed you so much."

"This place is amazing, and your opening was beautiful. Sammie, I'm so proud of you."

"Thank you, Zoë. That means a lot to me."

"Do you know how much you mean to me?" she asked.

"You mean a lot to me, too," I said.

"Sammie."

I looked at her.

"You thought I would just go back to Alex?"

"I don't know, but I knew that I didn't give you any reason to pick me."

She shook her head. She walked over and pulled me into her arms and squeezed me so tight. She pulled back and put her hands on each side of my face, "I picked you a long time ago, Sammie."

She kissed me with a passion that made my knees go weak.

I stood there for a minute, stunned and floaty at the same time.

"Wow. Umm, that was..."

"Yes, it was..." She smiled.

I cupped her face in my hands and kissed her back with as much passion.

"Okay, well..."

I stepped back and looked at her.

She laughed. "You better get back out there, Sammie. This is your big day."

"Not mine, ours! Let's go."

223

I grabbed her hand and walked to where everyone had gathered.

We all took a group on a tour of the community we built. To make each tour easier to conduct, the local Lions foundation had arranged five tractors with wagons. We started by showing them the barn we converted into a garden center and produce stand. The tractors took guests through the property which included the gardens and animals for therapeutic programs. Two rehab centers with twenty beds offered medical, psychological, drug, and alcohol treatment.

After forty days in the rehabilitation facility, the residents would move to a village of sixty tiny homes on the east side of the property. The café and coffee shop collaborated with vocational rehabilitation programs to hire residents.

On the south side of the property, there was a village of ten small homes that would be for families who were on their last step of transition into their own homes. The last thing we toured was the stables which held eight horses that would be used as part of the therapeutic programs for our residents.

As we finished, the crowd gathered around the stage again. I looked at Zoë.

She smiled and motioned for me to get up on the stage. I stood in front of the microphone stand once more.

"I hope you all enjoyed the tour."

The crowd applauded.

"We are honored to have you here with us on this important day. There are refreshments in the garden center, so please enjoy. Thank you all for coming and for your support in our community. I'm going to turn this over to Lexi now."

The crowd applauded again. I handed Lexi the mic and walked off the stage. Zoë was waiting for me at the bottom of the stairs.

†

Zoë and I mingled for a while, going our separate ways when a board member pulled me aside to talk. The day was nearing an end, and the crowd was dwindling. Zoë was talking to a board member. I stopped to tell her I was going to check all gates and doors to make sure they were locked. As I walked by the guys tearing the stage down, one of them stopped to let me know they would be back the next day to get the rest of the equipment.

I walked into the garden center. As I looked around, I couldn't believe it used to be the barn where I sat for hours, watching my grandpa putting something together. He would work on his old cars, whistling to the radio. I smiled when I thought of how proud he was of those cars and how much I loved spending time with him there. Zoë and her team of designers had done a wonderful job of re-creating the space. I was so grateful for her and her understanding of my vision.

A noise startled me. It felt like my heart jumped out of my chest. I turned around and saw the door at the back of the center was not closed all the way. They must've missed it earlier. It was weird someone would have opened it. I walked over to close it and got a strange feeling.

You're just being stupid.

I went out the front door, locked it, and headed for the stables to make sure all the stall doors and gates were secure. I loved that they could restore the old stables to the way they

225

looked when I was a kid. When I walked by the stall with the bay gelding, he came to the door.

"Hey, boy," I said.

He nudged me with his head. He reminded me of the horse Grandpa got for me after I moved in with my aunt. His name had been Tigger. I remember spending time with him in the same stables. I spent weekends, holidays, and part of my summer break with my grandparents, and I would go see him as soon as I arrived. He was my trusted companion, and he brought me comfort. I trusted this sweet boy to give to so many people that needed comfort and healing.

"Good boy." I patted his neck and walked toward the back of the barn to make sure all the slide bolts on the doors were secure. I heard a noise again but hesitated to look. My heart was racing. I turned around, and it was Zoë.

"Oh fuck, you scared me."

"Sorry babe, just checking to see if you need help."

"It's okay, I keep hearing things, but no one is there. It seems my imagination is playing games with me again."

"Let's get out of here. They invited us to Shorty's for a little celebration. Lanie is going to join us in about an hour. I told her I would drive Lexi over in her car, then she has someone dropping her off at the pub."

We walked out of the barn and toward the office.

"Sounds good. I just need to take a couple of things to the office, and then I'll be right behind you."

"I can wait," she said.

"No, go ahead. I'll be right there, I promise. Wherever you are is where I want to be." I winked at her.

She walked over to Lanie's car, and I walked into the office.

I put the keys in the desk drawer and locked the filing cabinets. I locked up the office, walked to my car, and got in.

"Oh shit," I mumbled to myself.

The gate remote. As I walked to the office, I realized the gate remote was in my pocket. I shook my head at myself and got back in the car.

As I drove to Shorty's pub, I wondered what my grandparents would have thought of Lexi's Place. I was sure they'd be proud and support the mission. It was their influence that drove me when it came to matters of the heart. Their kindness was always overflowing, and as a kid, I watched them commit acts of generosity that brought so much joy to people they didn't even know. I wanted to be like them.

I saw the sign for Shorty's and slowed down. The parking lot was full. There was an empty spot in the back, so I parked. I texted Zoë to let her know I was there and would be right in. I was so excited to spend time with her.

She sent me a happy face emoji. I got out of my car and started heading toward the back door of the pub. When I was about halfway to the door, I heard someone say my name. I didn't want to turn around, so I kept walking,

"Hey, are you ignoring me?" a male voice asked.

Oh my God, it was Brad.

I just kept walking, ignoring him.

He came running from behind a car and jumped in front of me. Panic hit me like a pile of bricks and paralyzed me with fear.

"Well, look at you, out here all alone."

I walked around him and just kept going. My body felt numb as the panic sat in.

He walked behind me. "Boy, you have all those people fooled, don't you? I wonder if they would think you are so fucking special if they knew where you came from and that you're a fucking queer?"

I kept walking, and he yelled, "Nothing to say, huh?"

I turned around, and he was leaning against a car as he took a drag of his cigarette.

"You were there? Why can't you just leave me alone?" I remembered thinking I saw him in the crowd but had dismissed it as my imagination. He started walking toward me, his eyes full of hate.

Why can't I move? I need to move, run...I need to run.

I recalled trying to run toward the back door of the pub. He grabbed the hair on the back of my head. I felt the burn as I pulled away with all I had, then I started kicking at him, swinging at him. My fists made contact with him as they were flailing through the air. He punched me in the face hard, knocking me to the ground. I quickly scrambled to my feet and tried to run again. He grabbed my arm, yanking me back around as he punched me in the face again and again.

I will not be his punching bag.

I kicked him in the knee, and he backed off for a second.

"You are such a dumb bitch, and you should have never pulled a gun on me and humiliated me like that in front of my friends."

"You shouldn't have raped me or gone after my friend," I yelled.

Another hard blow to my face almost put me down again, but I maintained my balance, and with every ounce of strength I had, I kicked him in the groin and stepped backward. He screamed out in pain and grabbed his crotch as he fell to the ground.

I started backing up faster until I stumbled over something and fell. I jumped up with no idea of where my glasses were. Everything was blurry.

I heard a POP.

My shoulder jerked back as something hit me hard. I instinctively turned around and started running.

Another POP.

I felt a sting in my left thigh as something hit it, making it hard to keep running, but I couldn't stop. I wouldn't let him win.

There was another POP.

Something hit the back of my knee, and then there was sudden excruciating pain. My leg gave out, and I hit the ground hard. I couldn't move; it hurt so much.

I heard people yelling and then POP...POP...POP.

"I got him," someone yelled.

I was on the ground. It was dark, and everything was blurry. Was this the end? Would I die? I had to do something, I couldn't let him win. I tried to get up, but someone put their hand on my shoulder and said, "Don't move. Help is on the way, ma'am."

There was the taste of blood in my mouth. My glasses were gone, and my eyes were nearly swollen shut—making it hard to see. I tried sitting up again, but I couldn't use my left arm, and my right leg was screaming from the intense pain.

Blurry figures ran toward me, and someone said, "Oh my God, that's Sam Wilson. Her friends are inside."

"Did someone call an ambulance? We need one for her right now."

"What about the shooter?"

"He's dead."

He's dead?

I closed my eyes. I could rest. He didn't win.

"Sammie, stay with me." I heard Zoë's voice.

"Zoë, you're here?"

"Yes, baby, I'm right here," she said.

She took my hand.

"What's wrong with me? Why can't I get up?"

"You've been shot, baby. Help is on the way."

A sudden queasy feeling came over me. *Shot? Did he shoot me?* I felt cold, but I was sweating. It hurt. Everywhere. My body trembled.

"We need a blanket," someone yelled.

"I have one in my car," another person called out.

Somebody covered me with a blanket.

"I got you," Zoë said. "They are almost here, baby."

I heard sirens.

I closed my eyes...I was so tired.

"Sammie, no, stay with me. Baby, I need you to stay with me." I heard her talking to me...then her voice faded...

Am I moving?

"Zoë!" I yelled out.

"I'm here, Sammie. They're going to take care of you. I'll be right here."

Who are they?

"Have you been hit, ma'am?" a male voice asked.

I heard Zoë say. "No, it's my girlfriend's blood."

Is it my blood...is it bad? I can't see it. Wait, did Zoë just call me her girlfriend?

I heard a man's voice. "We're transporting a female with GSW's to her left shoulder, thigh, and her right knee. She's losing blood and fading in and out of consciousness. Her blood pressure and pulse are steady but dropping. The patient is being treated for shock and received morphine and IV fluids. Patient is stable and in transit, five minutes out."

I'm so tired. I just want to go to sleep.

The last thing I remembered was Zoë telling me she loved me and needed me to stay with her.

Everything went dark.

CHAPTER EIGHTEEN

New Beginning

I wasn't sure how many days it had been since the shooting. Everything was fuzzy. There had been different doctors in and out of my room for days, but most of what they told me sounded a bit like Charlie Brown's teacher. Zoë was always there. She asked questions and wrote the things the doctor told her in a notebook.

A bullet shattered my patella and damaged my tendons and ligaments. After the surgery, the doctors believed a knee replacement was the best solution for me because of the amount of damage. The gunshot to my shoulder missed my artery, so I healed well with just some tissue damage. The bullet in my thigh stopped short of hitting my femur, and they removed it. Again, mostly tissue damage, but it would take some time to heal. The bruises on my face faded while the stitches mended the lacerations. I had two cracked ribs that were getting better, but were still tender to the touch.

The nightmares were vivid and frequent, and he was still alive in them. Sometimes I woke up crying and drenched in sweat. Zoë was always there to hold me and to remind me Brad was gone. But it was hard to wrap my mind around the fact that he was dead. It all seemed surreal sometimes.

They told me Brad was about to shoot me again when a security guard shot him. I never understood why he had so much hatred for me, enough to kill me. Never would I wish anyone dead, but he had given that guard no choice. Even though I knew he was dead, it wasn't easy to forget.

Zoë didn't leave my side. We were in a room that looked more like a hotel suite. There was a bed that came out of the wall. It completely messed with my head because I would wake up and there was a table and chairs. The next time, there was a small bed and a recliner next to mine, where Zoë sat every night to watch me breathe. One nurse told me when Zoë had gone to get a coffee that she never left my side.

One day I woke up, and we were talking when she said, "So, Natalie called earlier. You were asleep, and she didn't want me to wake you."

"Oh no, I'm sorry Zoë," I said.

"Don't apologize, it's okay. I told her I would let you know she called, and that is what I'm doing." She smiled.

"Thank you." I grabbed her hand and squeezed it. "You need to go home and get some rest. The nurses tell me you don't leave."

"That isn't true. I've gone home a few times. When the nurse I trust is on shift, I go home, grab more clothes, and water our plants. I take showers in this bathroom. It has a great shower. My laptop is here, and I check emails when you're asleep. I'm not leaving until you can come home with me."

"Aww, you are so sweet," I said.

"You think?"

"I know."

"So, how are you feeling?" Zoë asked.

"I'm okay. I'd be even better if you would come over here and snuggle with me," I said.

"Aww, of course I will."

She came over to the bed. I could tell she was hesitant to get into the bed with me. I slid over a bit and held my right arm up. "Come here."

She slowly got up on the bed and laid her head on my shoulder but struggled with where to put her arm.

"Sammie, I'm scared I'll hurt you," she said.

"Baby, I'm good. You can lay your arm across me."

She slowly put her arm across my body.

"Relax, babe, you're not hurting me, I promise." It felt so good to be next to her with her arm around me. I knew, with her, I would always be safe.

After a couple of minutes, Zoë looked at me.

"You're sure I'm not hurting you?" she asked.

"Yes, it feels good." I looked into her eyes. "Hey, why the tears?" I asked.

"Because I could have lost you that night to a deranged man."

"But you didn't...I'm right here."

"I know, and trust me, I'm so grateful for that. I'm not letting you go, ever."

"I don't want you to...ever."

"Good." She smiled.

We both fell asleep.

†

After two more surgeries, a knee replacement, and too much time in the hospital, they released me. I couldn't have been happier to be back in my own bed. Zoë was a wreck from worrying about me and making sure I was getting the best care. No matter how many times I told her everything was good and the care she gave was one hundred percent the best, she was still worried.

"Are you comfortable?" Zoë asked.

"Yes."

"You need anything?"

"All I need is you here with me and for you not to worry so much."

"I just want to make sure you're comfortable and can heal with no complications."

"I will. Now come over here and sit down for a while."

She came over, sat next to me, and I laid my head on her lap. All I wanted was to be close to her right now. Nothing else mattered to me.

She stroked my hair, and it felt so good.

"Let's get you to the bedroom. I need to change your bandage." She helped me sit up, walked over, grabbed the walker, and put it in front of me.

"I'm ready to lose this thing," I said.

"I know you are. It won't be much longer."

"I know. I'm grateful for your patience with me."

"You've been a good patient, and I love you."

"I love you back," I said.

She walked beside me, allowing me to be as independent as possible. As she was changing my bandage, we were just chatting. She looked up, and our eyes met. She smiled at me, and the feelings overwhelmed me. A tear hit my cheek.

"Sammie, did I hurt you?" she asked.

"No, not at all." I wiped the tear away. "They're good tears, I promise."

"Good." She winked at me. "So do you want to snuggle and watch a movie until dinnertime?"

"Yes, that sounds amazing."

✝

My recovery was coming along. The wounds were healing, and nightmares weren't as frequent. I had so much time to think about the life I had lived. After the first incident with Brad, I had tried to ignore my feelings and threw myself into my education and career. When my aunt found out I was "queer," it devastated her because her church friends were disgusted that she had a sinner living in her house.

My fears cost me time with the person who truly loved me. The inner voices told me I was not good enough for her. I stayed with someone I knew was not meant for me because her toxicity was what I was comfortable with. I wasted time running from the person who would always have my back. As I wrote my memoir, I realized I allowed many emotions, thoughts, and fears to drive me. Although I worked hard and made something of myself, I shut off parts of myself because I was afraid of what others would think. I wouldn't allow that fear to drive me anymore. I was going to live my life to the fullest. As I lay there in Zoë's arms, I smiled as she softly snored, and I realized I found it soothing. In the hospital, the only thing comforting me was being close to her and listening to her breathe. I loved her so much.

†

It had been months since the incident. My recovery had been going well, and thanks to the best doctor and physical therapist, I was walking again without assistance. Zoë continued to be by my side, and our connection continued to grow stronger. The walls no longer existed with her, and it was an amazing feeling.

One beautiful morning, we were sitting on the deck that overlooked the lake. Zoë found this place in Whitefish Bay while I was still out of it in the hospital. She wanted me to come home and heal in a place she knew would bring so much peace. She found a beautiful cottage on the shoreline. It was peaceful and serene. I had everything I ever wanted, including my person.

We went to visit Lexi's Place. I hadn't been there since the opening. I'd been told that Lexi had made a big impression on our board. Lexi's Place had the best administrative staff, teachers, counselors, and care staff. With the help of a generous community, dedicated board, and financial donations, this project made a difference in people's lives. I could not be prouder of what we all had accomplished together.

We pulled up, Zoë grabbed the remote, opened the gate, and we drove through. I couldn't believe how beautiful the flower beds were with all their blooms. We parked by the garden center. Zoë came around to open my door. She took my hand, and I got out. We walked over to the flower beds and I heard someone say, "Well, look who it is."

I turned around and saw Lou coming toward me.

"Hello Lou, how are you?" I asked.

She came up and gave me a bear hug. "I'm great," she said and stepped back. "Lexi is going to be so happy to see you."

"Where is she?" Zoë asked.

"The offices. I'll go get her," she said.

Lou walked away quickly to get Lexi.

"She looks great, so happy," I said.

"Yes, she's a sweet girl."

Lou worked in the garden center and took so much pride in her work. Her growth had been an amazing testimony of what someone can do with the right opportunities and resources. She wanted to get a degree in horticulture, so her team had worked endlessly to get her set up for success, and she had begun classes in the fall before Lexi's Place opened. She had an outstanding vibe, and I always believed she would reach her goals with the help of Lexi and her staff.

I heard Lou saying, "I told you she's here."

I turned around and saw Lexi walking toward me.

"Oh my gosh, Sammie, you look good."

"Aww. thank you. I have some weight to shed," I said.

"Whatever," Lexi said. She walked up and hugged me.

As we stepped back, I said, "So, I hear you've impressed the board."

"I don't know what you're talking about," she said. She tried not to smile.

"Girl, whatever. I see all the reports. Your numbers are very impressive."

"Well, that's because the brains behind it all made it easy."

"Stop it," I said. "So, take us on a tour."

"She still can't accept a compliment, can she?" Lexi asked.

"Baby steps," Zoë said as she smiled at me.

"I'm right here, ladies. Can we get on with this tour already?"

They both laughed.

Lexi said, "Give me a minute. I'll be right back to take you on that tour."

She came back on a golf cart and said, "Hop on, ladies."

"Nice," Zoë said.

I sat beside Lexi, and Zoë went in the back.

"The country club donated four of their carts to us when they got new ones. They're a huge blessing," Lexi said.

"Wow! What a great donation!" I said.

"Hold on, ladies."

Off we went on our guided tour. As we drove by the barn, I couldn't help but smile when I saw what I had envisioned when we were developing the property. Girls with grins grooming the horses, some preparing to ride. Their smiles said everything, and I knew exactly how much that meant.

The gardens were beautiful. Lou proudly waved at us from her spot amongst the tomato plants. It was all just a little surreal how this all came together. I was so happy that I survived that night to see this in living color. We drove by the single houses where independence blossomed. They decorated each little yard with flowers from the garden center. The ladies proudly displayed hand-painted ceramic birdhouses and garden elves in one yard.

The administrative staff had developed amazing programs. They taught parenting skills, living skills, and much more. The Department of Rehabilitation had an agency that oversaw and operated all our community businesses. It was exactly what I had hoped it to be.

"What are the tears about, Sam?" Lexi asked.

"Happy tears. You've all done such a fucking amazing job of bringing this all together and making our vision a reality." I took her hand and said, "I can't thank you enough for all you have done."

"Because of you, Sammie. It was your vision that made this happen, your heart and passion for others."

"We all did it together because we are survivors who have taken what happened to us and used it to help other people. We are unbreakable," I said as I squeezed her hand.

"I second what she said," Zoë added.

†

Fall was in the air. Originally, we had planned on heading south soon to avoid what winter brings to Wisconsin. Excitement, happiness, and overall greatness were present. We were living our best lives. We repurposed one bedroom in the cottage as an office for Zoë to manage two businesses and countless projects. Despite telling her I would be fine, she wouldn't leave me, so we traveled together ninety percent of the time. I planned on having my book finished by spring before returning to New Mexico.

The doorbell rang while I was busy responding to emails and calls in the office. I had just taken a call.

Zoë got up and whispered, "I got it."

I wrapped up my call, and when I turned around Zoë was standing by the door. She closed it slowly and turned around. She had a look on her face that I had never seen.

"Zoë, what's wrong?"

"Uh... Sammie, there is a woman in the living room that claims..." She paused.

"Who is she?" I asked.

"Sammie, she says she's your mother."

Mother?

I looked at Zoë. "What the fuck?"

She walked over to me and pulled me in her arms, and whispered, "I'm here for you, no matter what you decide. If you want me to go out and tell her to leave, that's what I'll do." She stepped back and looked at me. "You tell me."

"I'll go out there but don't leave me."

"Okay, baby, you got it."

Opening the door slowly, I walked out to the living room. There she was, sitting on the sectional couch. My mother. She looked so different.

She stood up and said, "Hi Sammie."

It kind of sounded like her. The voice was softer. Her eyes were different, not the color but the way she looked at me. What could she want now? I didn't know what to say. Nothing was coming out of my mouth. I just stood there.

"I hope this isn't a bad time," she said.

"Have a seat," Zoë directed.

She took my hand and led me to the other side of the couch, and we sat down.

"I heard about that man shooting you. I'm glad you're okay," she said.

I looked at her and asked, "What do you want?"

"That's a fair question." She went on, "I want to apologize for the way I acted when your grandma died. I was angry, and the things I did were wrong. I have no excuse."

"It started long before that, though, from the time I can remember."

"You're right. Everything I did was wrong. That person is dead. I'm a different person now."

She told us that after they took me away, she had a series of bad boyfriends, sold the property, blew all the money, and just lived with one drunk man after another. The drinking went on for years. She spent time incarcerated for DUIs. She was a no show for her father's funeral, and no one bothered to track her down. We would later find out it was one of the times she was in prison. It was the last time in that she finally turned things around. She got sober, and when they released her, she moved into a sober living house for a couple of years. She made some friends at the sober living house and got a job working with a veterinarian. At sixty years old, she moved into a three-bedroom house with two other ladies from sober living. She wasn't the same person she said, but why would I believe that?

"How did you find me?" I asked.

"You remember Kenny and Sue?"

"Vaguely."

"They live in the cottage next door. You know how people talk."

"So, what do you want with me?" I asked.

"I want you to know that I'm sorry for the things I did and for not being a mom to you."

"You hated me. I saw it in your eyes."

"I didn't hate you. I hated my life there and being married to your father."

"Why take it out on me? You hurt me. How could you do the things you did to me if you didn't hate me?"

"I was a selfish drunk, and I'll understand if you don't forgive me."

"Forgiveness happened a long time ago, but I will never forget the way you looked at me. I never felt safe or loved. You spent hours breaking me down, making me believe I was a bad kid and no one would ever love me? Why?"

"I didn't love myself, Sammie. I was a fucked-up person who tried to forget everything by drinking."

"But you made me feel unlovable. You told me so many times that no one would ever love me, that I was ugly and worthless."

"It's how I viewed myself, but you have been beautiful from the day you were born. You always did well in school. You're smart and beautiful, Sammie, and you have achieved great things, and I'm proud of you."

I felt so uncomfortable hearing her say those things. That was not what I was used to from her. Part of me wanted to crawl out of my skin. Zoë took my hand and gently squeezed it. I saw Mother's eyes go to our hands. I was waiting for a look of disgust to come over her face, but it didn't transpire.

"So, is this your roommate?" she asked.

"This is Zoë, and she's my girlfriend," I said.

I waited for her to say something ignorant.

"Well, that's nice. It's good to meet you, Zoë."

What is going on here? This woman is not the mother I remember.

"It's nice to meet you, too."

Wow, I couldn't have made this up. I would've never believed I would be in the same room as my mother, holding my girlfriend's hand. A woman that, from the first impression, was kind and soft-spoken. That was not who my mother was, never that I could recall.

"Would you be okay with having lunch with me tomorrow?" Mother asked.

I looked at Zoë.

"Zoë, you're welcome, too."

What? How is this possible?

"Where do you want to have lunch?" I asked.

"There is this hole in the wall just outside of Milwaukee. The food is good." She paused. "I can text you the address."

I just stood there, unsure of if I wanted her to have my number.

"Here, text it to me. She's driving, so I'll be navigating," Zoë said.

She wrote her number and gave it to my mother.

"Well, I'm going to get out of your way. I apologize for coming unannounced," Mother said.

"Okay, umm, we'll see you tomorrow at the hole in the wall," I said.

I saw my mother smile at us. She never smiled at me. It was weird. I didn't know how to act or react.

"See you tomorrow," she said as she walked out the door.

Zoë and I just stood in the middle of the living room, looking at each other. She reached out and wrapped her arms around me. In my safe place. I exhaled.

"You okay, Sam?" she asked.

"I honestly don't know how to react to what just happened. I don't know that person, and it was awkward as fuck to hear her talk like that. Her eyes are so different. There is no hate left. I don't know that woman."

"People can change, baby. Maybe she got sober, and she's different."

"How can I trust that?"

"One visit at a time, and I will always be there with you. We'll see how lunch goes and go from there. You're in control, baby. You make the calls."

I hugged her and whispered, "Thank you."

CHAPTER NINETEEN

My Happy Ending

Fall 2018

I was still trying to wrap my mind around the person who showed up at my house. She slightly resembled the woman I called Mother, but she was not the same person. She didn't act the same, look the same, or sound the same. Could people really change that much? I didn't know how to feel.

As we drove to the restaurant, my stomach flipped as my nerves went into high gear. It was a hole in the wall, just like Mother said. I hoped the food was as good as she claimed. She was waiting for us inside, and a server showed us to a booth. After we ordered food, Mother started talking about how she and her roommates had been following my work for years.

"We really like the article about that girl from Memphis. The one that you won the award for a couple of years ago," she said. "You're a gifted writer."

This was where I should've been saying thank you, but upon hearing something nice come from her mouth, my body froze. My mind stopped, and I literally couldn't process any of it. If not for Zoë, I would've probably been stuck on frozen. She grabbed my hand, bringing me back to the moment.

"Thank you," I finally got out.

Zoë held my hand, our fingers intertwined. I couldn't have done any of it without her. I looked at her and smiled. When I looked back at Mother, she was watching us. I couldn't help but wonder what she was thinking.

She started telling us about her job at the veterinary clinic. Her duty was to care for the animals that stayed overnight or post-surgery. She was proud of what she did at the clinic, and she seemed so happy. I had never really seen her happy, as I thought about it, not even when her friends were around. She was always getting into an argument with someone. In my memories, her eyes were always dark and carried so much hate. As I looked at her that day while she talked, I saw a twinkle in her eyes. She included Zoë in the conversation and seemed to like her, but Zoë wasn't hard to like. It was all so strange, like I was meeting someone I had never met before.

I told her about Lexi's Place hesitantly at first because I was uncertain if it would piss her off about the property being given to me. Zoë and I explained the different programs and how we had the animals and gardens.

"So you kept the old barns and garage?" she asked.

"Yes, and the house. Zoë's designers did an amazing job keeping the space original. The old garage is now the garden center, and they're using the old barns for the animals."

"Sounds cool," she said.

"Maybe you can come by sometime, and we can give you a tour," Zoë said.

"That would be great. I'd love that," she said.

We talked for a while longer, and then she said, "Well, girls, I need to get to the clinic." As she stood up, she grabbed the ticket to pay.

Zoë said, "Hey, leave that. We got it."

"Nope, I'm paying for it, and I will not argue with you. Thank you for coming to lunch."

She walked to the register and paid. Before she walked out the door, she waved at us one more time.

I looked at Zoë. "Who the hell is she?"

"Well, I never met the other version of her. What she did to you was very wrong. But the woman that we just had lunch with is kind of cool and funny."

"It's just so weird," I said.

†

It seemed like it was just opening day at Lexi's place. After the incident with Brad, everything was foggy, and time just passed. It was already October, and this would be the first time I was back since I was shot. I was excited to see everyone and all they had done. Zoë and I pulled up to Lexi's place. We were there to drop in on the Halloween Bash. Lexi put together a committee that was made of volunteers and women from the programs. She had been sending me pictures of them all laughing and working together. It was hands down the best Halloween party I had ever been to. It was fun watching the families celebrating together, dancing, and joining in on the games.

Zoë and I were watching the kids playing when I heard, "Hey, where are your costumes?"

We both turned around, and there was Lou, dressed as a witch.

"Hi, Lou. We aren't much into the costumes, but you look cute," I said.

"You don't like costumes? What's wrong with you?"

"Well..." I laughed and said, "We're just here for a bit to see what you ladies did to the place. It looks great. I'm getting some pictures for the newsletter while I'm here, too.

"You want a picture of me?" Lou asked.

"Of course," I said.

As I was taking Lou's picture, Lexi walked up and started talking to Zoë. I noticed Zoë show her something on her phone. Lexi looked at it and appeared to cover her mouth in awe. I walked up and said, "What are you girls looking at?"

"Oh, the picture of my niece I showed you earlier."

"She is adorable, isn't she?"

"She is," Lexi said.

"Well, of course, she takes after her aunt," Zoë said.

We laughed. I walked over to Lexi to hug her. "You guys put on a hell of a bash!"

"The ladies did this. It was fun watching them come together."

"I bet. They have an outstanding leader in you. I sleep well at night knowing that this place is in the best hands possible," I said.

"Aww thank you, Sammie."

"You're welcome." I gave her another hug. "You better get back to your party. We're going to head out."

"Thank you, ladies, for coming by," Lexi said as she hugged Zoë.

†

As we moved into November, the temperature dropped. The shore was still beautiful from the inside. The cottage we were renting had a fireplace. That was the best part of the cold weather. I ordered firewood when I found out we were staying for another winter. We would make use of the fireplace when the cold weather came.

I'd been working on editing the newsletter, the Christmas edition, for Lexi's Place. It needed to be ready for print for the first week in December. I continued to do my freelance work while I finished up my memoir. I was going to have dinner with my mother later. It'd be the first time I saw her without Zoë. Our visits had been pleasant so far, so I was hoping it would remain that way.

There was a conversation about the book that had to take place. She needed to know before I published. I included the abuse from my childhood in my memoir. The more I knew, the more I realized she was sick back then, addicted to that whiskey I had smelled too often. It didn't mean what she did was right. It did, however, change the way I viewed what happened. I realized it wasn't me she hated.

It was her life.

†

I arrived at the restaurant and met Mother. Luckily, it was not too busy yet, and we got seated in the back, where there would be less traffic. We ordered our drinks, and she asked, "Where's Zoë?"

"She's in New Mexico for work," I said.

Zoë had to fly to New Mexico for business for a week. She tried to get me to go, but I stayed behind to continue the work on my book. Although I had fallen in love with the shore again, I was ready to go back to New Mexico to begin life with Zoë, where it all began. Thanksgiving was coming up soon, it would be our first as a couple. We were going to go to Lexi's Place to serve the residents lunch, and then we were hosting a dinner for Lexi and her roommates.

"What kind of work does she do?"

"She has an interior design business she started right after college, and she inherited her father's real estate business a few years ago."

"Oh, that's good."

"Yeah," I said.

"She's a nice girl. I like her."

"Yeah," I said.

The server put the drinks down in front of us. We ordered our food, and then Mother asked, "What are you girls doing for Thanksgiving?"

"We're going to go serve lunch to the residents at Lexi's Place. Then we're having a small dinner at our place with Lexi and her roommates."

"That's nice," she said.

"You have any plans?" I asked.

"My roommates and I are cooking dinner, and some ladies from our group are coming over."

"That sounds nice."

"It will be. We like to play cards and stuff, it's fun. Do you guys need any more people to help serve? I would love to volunteer," Mother said.

"Yeah, I'm sure we can always use volunteers. I'll send the details."

"Okay."

The server brought our food out. We continued to chat in between bites. Once finished, I decided a conversation about the memoir needed to happen.

"So, I've been working on my memoir for months. I wasn't going to write it. When I first came to Wisconsin, I was staying in a house in Shorewood, and Aunt Marla showed up to visit. She brought up a lot of stuff from the past, which prompted me to visit the farm."

"What did she want?"

"I've no idea. She asked me if I could help her out when I told her she needed to leave."

"Wow, I haven't talked to her in years. I wonder what made her bring up that stuff."

"I don't know. When she brought up stuff with Grandpa and Grandma, I put a stop to it. She brought up the 'things' that happened."

Mother gave me a simple glance . "It's unfortunate that she showed up just to bring up the past, and I want to apologize for my behavior. I wish I could go back and change—"

I interrupted her. "No one can go back and change the past, but we can both overcome it."

"That is a good way to look at it," she said.

"Well, I didn't hold back on what happened on the farm. I just want you to know."

"I appreciate you letting me know. But the people in my life that matter know me and know my regrets about the things that happened in the past."

I still struggled with making eye contact with her, but I looked up briefly and then looked at my phone and said, "Well, there is no reason it can't have a happy ending."

†

Soon I would pick up Zoë from the airport, and I was happy about that. She told me there would be no more traveling back to New Mexico until we went together. That also made me happy because being without her had not been my favorite time. It had always been that way with Zoë. Spending time with her never got old. In fact, I felt like I had wasted so much time that could've been spent with Zoë. I wouldn't be wasting more time moving forward.

I pulled up to the airport and immediately spotted Zoë. I parked and got out of the car to help her with her bags. Mostly I wanted to hug her.

"Hey baby," she said as we hugged.

"I'm glad you're here," I said.

"Me too."

We got in the car, and Zoë said, "Damn, it is cold as fuck."

"Yes, it will only get colder." I laughed.

We got home, and Zoë was excited to make a fire. We brought some wood in, and I showed her how to use the fire starter bricks. As she got the fire started, I went to the kitchen to get us a glass of wine and some cheese and crackers. We both sat in an oversized chaise lounge and enjoyed the ambiance of our current settings. After a while, Zoë got up to add a log to the fire, and I refilled our glasses.

As I walked back into the living room, she asked, "How was dinner with your mother?"

"Weirdly good. I talked to her about the memoir, and she seems okay with it."

I handed her the glass of wine and sat down. She kissed me and said, "I'm so proud of you."

"For what? Getting our wine?" I said as I laughed.

"No, smartass." We both laughed more.

"Seriously though, Sammie, the way you have handled everything. Letting your mother back in, even though you didn't have to, and I feel like it's freed you."

"Yeah, I think you're right. I feel different."

We spent the rest of the evening enjoying our wine, the fire, and each other. I loved the life I had with Zoë.

†

After my grandma passed away, Christmas was not the same without her. I had holiday gatherings with friends and coworkers, but I always went home alone afterward and slept

Christmas day away. I remember one Christmas before Grandma got sick. We went to this place that was kind of like the North Pole, and it was so magical. Tall, decorated trees, carolers, and elves. It was my favorite Christmas. I had never experienced another like it.

That year Zoë and I decorated our temporary home. We went to the Christmas tree farm to get an actual tree. We danced to Christmas music around the cottage, went to see the Nutcracker ballet in Milwaukee, and braved the cold to witness the Christmas parade. We wanted to experience a white Christmas and sledding in the park together. Zoë wanted to go ice skating, but it was a hard pass for me. She walked away from her experience on the ice with no broken bones. We were enjoying the holiday season for sure.

One evening after dinner, Zoë was making a fire. When I walked into the living room, she looked at me and said, "So, I have a bit of a surprise for Christmas Eve."

"Oh, you do? What is that?" I asked.

"I rented a space downtown for Christmas Eve."

"A space?"

"Yeah, well, we are hosting our first Christmas Eve party."

"Oh, are we?" I asked.

"Yes, don't kill me, please."

"Why would I kill you?"

"Well, I invited some people, like my family, your cousin, his family, and your mom."

"Oh my God, what the hell are you thinking?"

"That I love you and want you to have the best Christmas ever."

"I don't know how my mother and your family will get along, and I don't know how Brandon feels about seeing her," I said.

"I talked to Brandon, my family, and your mom," she said.

"You have it all worked out, huh?"

"I do. I just need you to be there, and everything will be perfect."

"I wouldn't be anywhere else."

It seemed like we had a party to attend every other day. We flew to New Mexico to attend work parties the weekend before Christmas. The holidays were becoming exhausting. Although I loved celebrating with Zoë, I was ready for them to be over with. It was Christmas Eve Day and it seemed a little hectic as we tried to get ready for the party. Zoë was in and out of our room. I heard her on the phone talking to someone about tonight. She seemed kind of nervous. Zoë always wanted the party she hosted to be perfect, so I was sure that was why she seemed anxious. She walked back into the room.

"Hey," I said.

"Yeah, babe."

"You need a hug?"

"From you, always." She walked over and hugged me.

"Everything is going to be perfect tonight, and you look so hot."

She squeezed me and then stepped back and said, "So do you, babe."

"Thank you, and don't worry, baby," I said as she walked out of the room again.

I saw her pacing back and forth in the living room as she talked on the phone. I wondered what she was not telling me. Maybe something was going on with her family or the business. I was sure she would fill me in later. For now, I needed to finish getting ready, so we weren't late.

As I walked to the kitchen, Zoë was texting as fast as she could. It was usually me who was a ball of nerves, especially since my mother was going to be at this party. I didn't know how I felt about it. I knew how important the party was to Zoë, so I wasn't going to let anything, or anyone ruin our Christmas Eve.

Zoë walked over to me and took my hand. "You ready?"

"Yes."

As I drove to the party, I noticed that Zoë's leg was bouncing fast. I reached over and put my hand on her leg. We looked at each other, smiled, and I said, "I don't know what has you so anxious, baby, but it's going to be perfect because we're going to be there together."

"Yes, indeed," she said.

We pulled into the parking garage as close to the elevator as possible because it was so cold outside. We walked hand in hand to the elevator and up to the party. When we walked into the room, I gasped.

Zoë took my coat and asked, "Do you like it?"

"It's beautiful Zoë. There are live musicians and carolers, too?"

"Yes, all of that." She leaned in and kissed me. "All for you."

"I love you. Did you invite everyone we know?"

"I love you, too, and yes, I did." She smiled and asked, "You ready to mingle?"

"Yes, I'm ready." I winked at her, and we headed toward the group.

We saw her mother and walked over to talk to her. Zoë's mom had been super sweet to me since I met her. She had always supported Zoë, and even though they occasionally butted heads over the business, they had a great relationship.

Zoë's brother and wife walked up, and we chatted with them for a little while.

I saw my cousin and his family walk in. We walked up to them, and I hugged Brandon. Then his son ran up to me and hugged my legs tight while yelling, "Sammie! I miss you."

"Aww, I miss you too, buddy. We'll be home soon."

I hugged his wife and kissed their beautiful baby girl on the cheek. It was good to see all of them again. The kids were growing so fast. I looked over and saw Zoë talking to a couple of ladies.

Brandon asked, "Sam, is that your mom?"

"Yes, it is, and roommate."

"Wow," he said.

Zoë walked over with the ladies. I looked at Brandon, and I could tell it shocked him to see her. As they approached, it got awkward until Zoë said, "I found these two flirting with the elves."

Both ladies started laughing. "That's not true," they said at the same time.

Zoë was absolutely the best at breaking the ice, one of the many things I loved about her. Everyone seemed comfortable. Lexi came over with Lou, and they both hugged me and Zoë.

"You look so good, Sammie," Lexi said.

"Yeah, what she said," Lou said.

"Thank you, ladies," I said.

We had a lot of different Christmas snacks and drinks of all sorts. People were laughing, enjoying each other, and dancing while the band played our favorite Christmas songs. The party went on for some time before Lexi walked up to the small stage and told the band to take a break. She grabbed a mic and said, "Hey everyone, can I get your attention for just a moment?"

Suddenly, the room got quiet.

"Thank you! So, I just wanted to say a couple of things, and then we can get back to the party." She paused and said, "First, I want to thank Zoë for this beautiful gathering. You knocked it out of the park, my friend."

The group applauded.

"Sammie and Zoë, can I get you two to come up here, please?"

I whispered, "What the fuck?" Zoë took my hand, and we walked up to the stage.

"Sammie, I know you're not a fan of being in the spotlight."

I nodded in agreement.

She promised to keep it short and then noted the joy of being surrounded by so many wonderful people for the holidays. She turned to me.

"About twenty minutes from here, families are celebrating the holidays together. They are sober, safe, warm, and united with their families again. Marking a future that was made possible by your vision, Sammie. You two rock everything you do. I'm so happy to have you both in my corner. Thank you for all that you have done for me and our community. That's all."

The group applauded.

Oh, thank goodness, that was short and sweet. We both hugged Lexi, and I turned to walk back to the group when Zoë asked, "Sammie, can I get you to stay with me for a minute?"

"Okay," I said.

She took the mic from Lexi, came back over to me, and took my hand. "Come with me."

I followed, and we stopped in front of the giant Christmas tree. She let go of my hand and said into the mic, "Merry Christmas, everyone."

"I wanted to thank you all for coming tonight and spending your Christmas Eve with us." Zoë looked at me and grabbed my hand again.

"Most of you know that this is our first Christmas Eve together, as a couple," Zoe amended. "And we wanted to share it with all of you. Thank you to our families from New Mexico for flying up to the frigid cold to celebrate with us." Everyone laughed and agreed it was cold.

Zoë turned toward me, squeezed my hand, and whispered, "I love you."

She turned back toward the group. "As many of you know, this girl has had me chasing her for years, but rejection didn't stop me..."

The group said in harmony, "Aww."

I shook my head and smiled.

"It's okay. She was worth the wait," she said as she waved her hand and turned toward me again. "Sammie, I just want to say thank you for letting me in and trusting me with your heart. You deserve nothing but the best, to be loved the same way you love, unconditionally and without limits. You are such an amazing person. It would be my honor to grow old with you."

The next thing I knew, Lexi walked up, and Zoë handed her the mic and went down on one knee.

"Samantha Grace Wilson, I fell in love with you a long time ago, and I have waited for the day that you would let me love you. I'm glad it's here, and I hope you will give me the honor of making you, my wife."

Oh my God, is this real? Or am I dreaming?

I looked at her. Everything paused at that moment.

"Before you answer, just know that I got down on one knee for you. Now I'm going to hope that you say yes, but if you say no, well, I'm going to need your help with getting up either way."

Everyone laughed.

I smiled and said, "I got you."

She opened the box. "Please say yes," she said.

I lost it. I leaned down, took her face in my hands, kissed her, and whispered, "Oh my God, Zoë. Yes, yes, of course, I will."

I helped her stand up, and she put the beautiful ring on my finger.

She turned to everyone, held my hand in the air, and yelled, "She said yes."

The room came alive, the lights, the music, and the elves dancing around. Our friends and family were clapping and cheering.

"I love you, baby," she whispered.

I hugged her tight. "I love you too."

Lexi came up and hugged both of us and then said into the mic, "Okay, thank God that is over. I don't think I could have taken another day of Zoë's nerves." Everyone laughed.

"I wanted it perfect," she said.

"This explains a lot. I thought you two were being weird."

We all laughed.

Lexi continued, "Seriously though, I'm so happy for the two of you. Congratulations!"

We walked away, and the band started playing again. I stopped and turned toward her. "Zoë, I didn't think this day could get any better. This room is magical with everything you know I love. You just made it the best day of my life." I kissed her.

"You deserve it all," she whispered.

"Thank you." I hugged her close. I felt someone put their arms around both of us.

"I'm so happy for you two, and I get another daughter," Zoë's mom said.

We all hugged and chatted for a minute before I heard, "Congratulations."

I turned around to see Brandon and his family. We all hugged again. They told us they were headed to the hotel to get the kids to bed because they were going to his mom's in the morning.

My mother walked up to us. "Congratulations, you two."

"Thank you," I said.

"Zoë, thank you for inviting me."

"Of course," she said.

I turned toward Lexi, and my mother grabbed my arm. Knee jerk reaction was to pull away and get in defense mode, but I stopped.

"Sammie," she said.

I turned toward her and said, "Yeah."

"Give me a hug." I leaned in awkwardly, and she put her arms around me. My arms were there somewhere, but I couldn't feel them. This was not normal. I looked at Zoë. Who knows what my face looked like.

She winked and smiled. I didn't know how to act. My mother had never hugged me a day in my life, and it felt very awkward. She let go and said, "We're going to head home. Thank you again for the invite. Merry Christmas."

"Merry Christmas," I said back.

"I'm so happy for you, Sammie, and proud of the person you have become."

"Thank you."

She walked away with her friend.

I just looked at Zoë. She hugged me and said, "I love you."

"I love you, too."

Lexi walked over and put her arm around me.

"Come with me for a minute, please."

"What are we doing?" I asked, suspiciously.

"I have something for you."

We walked into the room where our coats were, and she pulled out a neatly wrapped box. I opened it and, it was a beautiful crystal sculpture, and engraved on the base was, *Let me tell your story and let's make it a happy ending.*

SGW

"Oh my gosh, it's beautiful, Lexi. Thank you."

"You're welcome."

She smiled at me. "I remember the day we met. You told me I mattered. No one had ever said that to me. You told me my story was important. You told Lou that she could make her story have a happy ending. Those words have stayed with me. I remember that day and how I thought to myself, *why does she care?*"

She paused as she took both of my hands and held them tight.

"Sammie, you have stood by me more than anyone in my life. You are the sister I always wanted and the friend I never thought I could have. You believed in me and made me believe that despite everything that happened, I could have my happy ending." She wiped away a tear and said, "Today I got to witness you getting your happy ending. There is no one I know that deserves it more."

"Thank you, my sweet friend," I said.

We embraced.

ABOUT THE AUTHOR

MIA BARNES

Mia Barnes spent nearly two decades empowering others in a rewarding career. By empowering others, she found the strength to pursue her dream of writing and earned her Master's in English and Creative Writing. Although she has been writing for years, it was during grad school that Mia discovered a love of fiction writing. As a sapphic author, she likes to create robust characters to tackle different social issues—past and present. When Mia isn't working on a project, you can find her hiking with her German Shepard or kayaking with her partner and friends.

OTHER AFFINITY BOOKS

Mom's Last Wish by Charlene Neil

After fifteen years away from home, Lucy Donald receives an email from her mother's personal assistant, Cameron Bishop, compelling her to return. Soon after Lucy's arrival, threatening letters start to appear, and Lucy realizes her life is in actual danger. She seeks comfort in the arms of the alluring Cameron Bishop, but can Cameron really be trusted?

Lucy's return home and the events that unfold lead to an intense and suspenseful atmosphere.
Left to uncover the mysteries by herself, she finds herself grappling with the dilemma of not knowing whom to trust.

The Next Generation by Annette Mori

Despite Toni's legendary brilliance, even she could not stop the march of time. After learning her daughter, Joy, and Joy's two best friends, Pepper and Alina, attempted to deceive the senior agents in The Organization with a bogus

Spring Break cover story, she convinces her wife it's time to let the Next Generation take over.

The last thing Pepper Maggio expects after agreeing to lead a mission is literally running into the woman she's followed for years. Not only is Grace Turner beautiful, but she's a passionate crusader for the same innocents that The Organization vows to protect. Along with her two best friends, the three young women embark on an adventure to save the day. But the mission quickly gets out of hand as the human traffickers target not only Grace and her film crew, but also the young Mexican woman who managed to catch Alina's eye. Maria might be the bravest of the bunch as a survivor of one of the Mexican mines, but she's a sitting duck if they don't intervene. They might be the Next Generation, but they'll need the full support of The Organization, including Pepper's lethal mother, Val, to get out of Mexico alive.

<u>Turn the Page by Ali Spooner</u>
Continue the journey with Whit and Eli in this final installment of the Cast Iron Farm series. The brilliance of their twins, Mack and Zack, rapidly develops, challenging Whit and Eli to keep up with their education. Their sensitivity to others and kindness are far beyond their youth and a testament to the family's efforts to help them grow into young adults. In addition to more adventures, a budding romance, and wedding bells ring for the Fortner family once more as a new generation begins life on Cast Iron Farm.

A Breath of Scandal by S Anne Gardner
Adele Visconti, Contessa de Caravagio, is passionate and wild and doesn't know the meaning of the word no. One day by chance she turns her head and in a very old cliché fashion she sees a face across the expanse of a Polo field and goes to meet it. Unknowingly this would change her life forever.

When Gillian meets Adele, she is in a committed relationship. The last thing she wanted was to be sucked into the maelstrom that is Adele. However, Adele was something that she could not fight against and her world was turned upside down from the moment they met.

Will their relationship survive against a tide of intrigue, manipulations, passion, family, and most importantly reconnecting the magic of their love for each other.

The Sky People by Ali Spooner
After a beautiful wedding, Eli and Whit return to plan the next phase of their relationship. Whit discovers the identity of her father, and he shares a future with her that will change life on Cast Iron Farm forever. Twins bless the Fortner family, and Eli shares a special secret with Mitch, who bonds with the children in a unique way. Ride along as the Fortners begin a new chapter of their story.

Love Bonds by Annette Mori
When Mila Thompson, a rookie police officer, discovers her mother is missing, she engages the assistance of San Diego's number one detective, who is more than a

little reluctant to enter the fray, noting she works in homicide, not missing persons.

Bernie doesn't play well with others, which is why she doesn't have a partner at work or in her personal life. When Mila approaches her, she tries hard to refuse the request, but Mila will not accept no for an answer. For reasons she does not understand, Bernie doesn't want to say no to Mila, who can charm her way into anything, including smoothing the rough edges of Bernie's crusty heart.

Things get complicated when the women in The Organization have an unusual tie to Mila's mother. This sets up an action-packed adventure with twists and turns and a healthy dose of love. Find out the future of The Organization and whether an unlikely pair can find their way to love.

Holy Water and Whiskey Scars by Ali Spooner
Faith Wilson and Logan Bronson have family secrets to protect and a legacy to uphold to support their small rural Appalachian community. Their commitment to each other is strong, and their desire to aid the struggling families however they can, lead them both down an exciting but dangerous path. Will their love continue to grow and be the glue that binds the community together, or will they flee the withering community?

Politics of Love by Annette Mori
Governor Sandra Murphy is rethinking the sanity of allowing her mother to talk her into considering becoming the democratic party's choice for the presidential nominee. Sandra has enough to contend with after surviving a bomb

attack, thanks to the brave border control agent working alongside the clever undercover FBI agent. Now she has to worry about a pesky reporter who seems to be everywhere scoping stories Sandra would prefer Wynter Holmes steer far away from.

Wynter admires the charismatic governor. After all, she voted for the woman. But that doesn't give Governor Murphy a free pass. A breaking story is what Wynter lives for, and she isn't about to stop digging just because the engaging governor is attractive, single, and an out lesbian. Reporting for the famously biased, right-wing media conglomerate is not exactly making Wynter a friend of the enigmatic leader.

Will repeated attempts on Governor Murphy's life where Wynter might be collateral damage bring them closer together or tear them apart from what might be a perfect match?

Out and Loud by Ali Spooner

The Bentleys have begun celebrating their success by performing live in small venues and outdoor concerts. Their music and love for one another continue to grow as their number drops to four. Stone is needed at home to run the business during his father's rehabilitation, but the Bentleys drive forward. Cedra's challenge to her bandmates to create original songs for their next album turns into brilliant love songs, rockabilly, and a Pride Festival anthem. Ride along with the Bentleys as they capture the hearts of country music lovers across the nation.

Undercover Love by Annette Mori

When the domestic terrorist cell Emma Schmidt has infiltrated summons her to an abandoned warehouse for a loyalty test, Emma immediately recognizes the battered woman. Emma must act fast to protect her cover and save the woman, Jimena Aguilar, she's never forgotten.

Emma and Jimena team up on a dangerous mission to take down the terrorist cell and save the life of the popular California governor.

Will this lead them back to the closeness they once shared or have the years in between hardened their hearts to love.

Changing Times by Jen Silver

Thirty years on from when we first met Dani Barker and Camila Callaghan in *Changing Perspectives*, they're enjoying marriage and semi-retirement in a luxury flat near London.

Dani's niece, Holly, runs their mixed media business, now gaining a foothold in the highly competitive online games market. Holly's older sibling, Luc, influences people to take action on climate issues with their website, Gaia One: One Earth, One Chance.

Romance has been in short supply for both Holly and Luc. Immersed in her work, Holly's dating life is non-existent. For Luc, family prejudices stand in the way of a relationship with the love of their life.

Can Holly and Luc succeed in making the changes necessary to achieve their own happy ever afters?

Affinity
Rainbow Publications

eBooks, Print, Free eBooks

Visit our website for more publications available online.

https://affinityebooks.com/

Published by Affinity Rainbow Publications
A Division of Affinity eBook Press NZ LTD
Canterbury, New Zealand

Registered Company 2517228